THE H

The Haunting of Susurrous Pines

Jennifer Warmuth

Chapter One

The Unexpected

The investigation led them to a dense forest located in a mountainous region on a frigid day in late Autumn. Prepared as they were, Jillian and James were surprised by the quick turn of the weather. They scrambled to gather all the gear in the middle of the night to start the long hike down the mountain and back to the parked car. The snowfall picked up quickly and they found themselves hiking in the dark, cold, wind, ice, and snow. The ice was pelting their faces and Jillian's glasses continued to smear with ice and water making it more difficult to see. After wiping the water off her glasses enough times, she gave up and placed them in her pocket. They used flashlights that helped minimally as the light reflected off the falling snow. They could only see the immediate path in front of them as they walked. The focused light in the thick snow on such a dark night with the strong wind blowing created a visual tunnel effect. Jillian and James mapped out the path at the beginning of this trip and were following an old established hiking trail. They were both experienced at hiking and camping and understood the dangers of hiking at night in these conditions. With this snowstorm, the trail was barely distinguishable and they could easily become disoriented. Mags ran ahead leading the way and seemed to be the least inconvenienced by this surprise storm.

The hike became more challenging as the snow accumulated on the ground and the wind became stronger. The visibility continued to decrease and after a while, James was unsure if they were still following the trail. He hoped they were heading in the right direction as they trudged on. Mags continued to run ahead, and James depended on her to accurately guide them as she usually did. Jillian started to shiver as her clothes became soaked through. Next time they would make sure to bring snow gear even if it was early in the season-she thought to herself.

Her hands were red and freezing and her face felt numb. James realized if they did not quickly find the car, they might find themselves in serious trouble.

As uncomfortable as they felt, Jillian could not help but comment on how beautiful the snow was as it fell around them. It was so quiet they could hear the snow landing on the trees, the leaves, and the ground and she could identify the different sounds it made when it landed on the various surfaces. James said, "Jillian you can always find the silver lining." They plodded along stepping carefully in the deepening snow. Jillian rounded a bend and heard a loud crack abruptly breaking through the silence. She pointed her flashlight above her and could see a large branch breaking off a thick tree trunk and she screamed for James to get out of the way. "James watch out! A huge branch is coming down!" James ran off the trail just in time as the branch started to fall hitting other branches along the way. It landed with a loud thud and Jillian ran over to him to make sure he was ok. He was sitting down in the snow after losing his footing. He said, "I am fine thanks to you." "You were so focused on the sounds you noticed the tree branch before I did." Jillian gave him a hug and helped him back to his feet. They gathered themselves and continued the hike walking carefully around the fallen limb.

After about an hour of difficult hiking, James spotted the car with his flashlight. Mags ran ahead and stopped at the car and Jillian breathed a sigh of relief. She was starting to feel genuinely concerned they might become lost in the worsening conditions. After brushing the snow off the car, they dumped the gear in the back, loaded Mags in the back seat area, and started down the mountain. James turned up the heat and they spent a few minutes trying to warm up. Jillian said, "Well, we are sitting in soaked clothes but at least we have heat."

They had a long drive down the mountain and there were no other cars around. The quiet and solitude although at times sought after were not welcome on this night. It was eerie to be so far from the nearest town late at night in such a storm. The car they drove was a small SUV and James hoped it would get them down the mountain. Mags was curled up on the back seat comfortably sleeping and peacefully unaware of the dangerous driving conditions.

James drove slowly down the steep hills and around the sharp turns and curves as they made their way down the mountain. The fog was developing and visibility was worsening, and the road was covered with snow and ice. The headlights from the car created more reflection and glare when it hit the falling snow. James focused intensely on the road ahead, squinting as he tried to see the road through the fog, snow, and glare. They were completely isolated without seeing a single car on the winding road. James drove around a very sharp curve and the car started sliding on the ice. He yelled, "Hold on!" and before Jillian knew what was happening, they were sliding into an embankment. The car hit the rocks covered with snow along the embankment with a loud bang and then all was silent. They both paused for a moment realizing they had just crashed the car. The car was running, and the headlights were still on and shining through the thick falling snow. They pushed the car doors forcefully to open them and stepped out to look at the damage. James got back into the car and tried to back out onto the road. The car was hopelessly stuck with the front and sides severely damaged. They grabbed their phones to call for help. Mags ran around playfully sniffing and inspecting around the car.

Jillian looked down at her phone and looked up again when she thought she heard an unusual noise. She turned her head in the direction of what sounded like music but the noise was faint like a whisper. James started to say something, and she said, "Shush for a minute. I thought I heard a noise." They both stood quietly listening in the darkness. The soft sound of snow falling and hitting the ground was the first noise they could hear. As they concentrated, the faint sound of music could be heard in the distance. James said, "I hear it and it's coming from right over the edge." They both stepped carefully over the embankment next to their car and could hear the music more clearly. Jillian took her flashlight and pointed it in the direction of the sound. She could see another car covered in snow located down the cliff from their car. "James I can see a car and it looks like it went off the road and wrecked on the cliff." The car was precariously perched on a small level area on the side of the mountain near the edge of a cliff. The cliff was very steep, and the bottom was an exceptionally long way down. Jillian looked at Mags and told her to stay as Mags stood on a grassy area a safe distance from the road. Mags sat and watched curiously as James and Jillian urgently started the difficult hike down the rocky and snow-covered cliff area to see if anyone needed help. With flashlights they stepped carefully in the dark, hiking down the steep mountainside grabbing tree branches and holding on to rocks along the way. It was a challenging hike down the mountain in the darkness with such low visibility, and with the snow and ice covering most surfaces. Finally, after what seemed like an exceedingly long time, they reached a more level area of terrain and were able to run over to the car.

As they approached the car the music was playing loudly. The car had rolled and was now upright with the roof partially crushed. They pointed flashlights inside the car and could see two people slumped over in the front seats. Jillian was standing on the driver's side as James tried to open the passenger side. James took the phone out of his pocket and called 911. He explained the situation when he reached the police. The police stated they would send help as soon as possible but due to the weather, it might take a while. James ended the call and tried to open the passenger's door again. He could see the passenger was injured and bleeding.

Jillian tried repeatedly to open the driver's side door with no success. She tried to force the door open pushing on the side of the car with her foot for leverage to no avail. The snow was still coming down and the darkness did not help. She tried calling out to the people inside the car with no response. James yelled out that he was opening the passenger door. It would not open fully but he could carefully pull the person out. He gently took hold of the person by the shoulders and pulled them out of the car and into the snow. It was a man in about his mid-twenties and he had a serious head injury. James checked for a heartbeat and could barely hear one. He knew this man was gravely injured.

Jillian asked James if he could help her pull the driver-side door open. He ran around the car to her side, falling as he slid in the snow. He joined her and together they were able to pull the door open. The door creaked and groaned as they forced it open. Immediately Jillian covered her mouth with her hands and let out a muffled scream. The man in the driver's seat was gravely injured and appeared to have part of the steering wheel embedded in his chest. They both understood instantly he had little chance of surviving. As they looked at him feeling helpless, his eyes shot open. Jillian and James jumped in surprise. He looked at them wide-eyed and tried to speak. His voice was weak, muffled, and raspy and he said, "Don't let me die, I can't die tonight." They looked at one another understanding he was unlikely to survive the serious injuries. He attempted to move and started to panic, slowly realizing his situation. Jillian tried to calm him down telling him help was on the way. He looked at her again and said, "I cannot die please don't let me die tonight." She looked at James with tears in her eyes. They could not help him and hoped that when EMS arrived, they might be able to save him.

It was at that moment after the injured driver begged for them to save him that Jillian noticed the aura. This man had a developing aura of color around him that was becoming more vibrant. It was not the aura that concerned Jillian since she was accustomed to seeing auras. It was the changing colors. The colors of an aura had important meaning and the color she was looking at was extremely ominous. She had never seen such a brilliantly red aura around a person. As she was observing this bright red aura it was dynamic and in motion. While she was observing this aura vibrating and pulsating, the man in the car made eye contact with her. In a low guttural voice, he whispered, "Why are you wasting your time with this person when you need to be speaking with me?" She jumped back and bristled at the sound of this voice. This voice was completely different. It was deep and raspy and had an inhuman tone. As she stood there frozen in her tracks he spoke again. This time, in a panicked, weak voice that better matched his appearance and was consistent with the first voice he spoke with, he quietly said, "It is here. We made a mistake, and it is here." Jillian immediately felt sympathy for this man. He was expressing remorse, realizing his predicament. She also regretted terribly that she was not able to help him more. He was sitting there in the seat, trapped by the steering wheel and possibly by other injuries he might have. He must have been in terrible pain.

Jillian tried to keep the conversation going. She understood she might be the last person he ever speaks with. It was important for her to listen carefully to what he had to say. She asked, "What do you mean by It's here?" "What mistake did you make?" The man paused and then groaned. He seemed suddenly overwhelmed by pain. He said, "Please help me. I need to get out of this car." Jillian answered, "We have called for help, but it may take emergency services a while to get here due to the weather. It will be ok. We will stay with you both until they arrive. He looked down at his chest and moaned again. Jillian felt tortured by the situation and the inability to help this man. She looked in the back of the car and could see a blanket. She reached back and grabbed the blanket and draped it around the man. In the back of her mind, she was also feeling preoccupied with the ominous, inhuman voice she heard. That familiar voice.

James was back on the other side of the car trying to save the passenger stretched out in the snow. He discovered the man had a serious leg wound and he was using a piece of torn cloth to wrap around the leg to slow down the bleeding. As he was wrapping the leg the man opened his eyes and James found himself transfixed in the injured man's gaze. The man said, in a low raspy voice, "Help me." James was stunned and as he hesitated to respond, the man let out a last breath and his eyes took on a glazed appearance. James checked for a heartbeat and could no longer hear one. He tried to perform CPR repeatedly with no success. He sat down in the snow next to the man. He was out of breath, and exhausted, feeling frustration and overwhelming sadness. Emergency services would arrive too late to help this man.

Jillian stood in awe transfixed, watching this brilliant red aura float around the severely injured driver. She was trembling from the adrenaline and stress and as she watched she was jolted out of the trance by the sound of dripping and the strong smell of gas. She immediately understood the imminent danger and screamed for James. James jumped up and ran around the car and she said, "Listen, I hear dripping. Do you smell the gas? This car may catch fire or explode." They both looked through the open car door at the driver slumped over the steering wheel. Then they heard the sound of fire and flames. The noise of flames hissing, licking, catching, and growing could be heard getting louder. Within seconds the fire was visible and before they could react the entire car was engulfed in flames. The driver picked up his head and screamed and Jillian could see the brilliant red aura mixing with black and becoming larger as the car became a fireball. Jillian and James turned and started to run. They were thrown off their footing when the car exploded. They both were falling and tumbling down the cliff until they could grab a rock or tree branch to stop the fall. Jillian fell farther down, and James called out to her to make sure she was safe. She called back saying she was all right. She had found footing and grabbing a branch helped to stop her fall. They both rested for a few moments before attempting the climb back up the cliff. Flames, embers, and car parts that exploded into the air were falling and landing in the snow all around them.

James yelled, "Cover your head, there is falling debris!" Jillian leaned over and hid her head under a thick bush growing from the side of the cliff, while James placed his hands over his head. They waited a few minutes for the debris to stop falling and then continued the climb back up the cliff. It was steep and perilous. James made it up to the area where they found the wrecked car. He grabbed Jillian's hands as she climbed up near the cliff area where he stood. He carefully pulled her up the steep edge. Breathing hard and sweating in the cold, they both stayed sitting on the ground for a few minutes. When ready they stood up and were now standing next to the smoldering car. What was left of the car was blackened with billowing smoke. The front end of the car was destroyed and there was no sign of the man who was injured in the driver's seat. The man James tried to help was still on the ground and partially covered in snow and debris. They surveyed the scene feeling dread and sadness. Jillian thought about the families of these men. The unexpected and horrible calls the families were going to receive about the accident. She sighed, feeling her head pound. James held his head and rubbed the sides of his face. His ears were ringing due to the loud noise from the explosion. His hearing was impaired and the sounds around him were muted as if he had thick cotton stuffed in his ears.

It was dawn now, and the snow had stopped. The sun was just showing over the horizon lighting the valley below. James could hear commotion from above. Mags was barking and he heard the engines and could see the flashing red lights from EMS vehicles. He heard people on the road from above and James started yelling, "Down here, we are down here!" A few EMS people peered over the edge of the road and could see the burned-out, smoking car. They called out to Jillian and James letting them know help was on the way.

Chapter Two

The Mystery of Auras and Dreams

It began sometime after the haunting experience at the Edin house so many years ago. The visions started as a gray misty glow encapsulating people usually in times of high stress. The more upset or angry a person became the more the aura was visible. Jillian learned this was the result of increased energy release due to the strong emotions, although she did not understand the exact mechanisms behind this process. Initially, she did not see this experience as anything unusual and assumed everyone could see auras. As time continued and she was discovering her abilities, the auras she would see around people became increasingly more vibrant and colorful. She realized after talking with people that she was in fact the only person she encountered who could see these colorful auras. Jillian learned the meaning of these visions, and how to understand these colors over time and experience. She developed a color code to understand more about what she was seeing. This ability to see auras became an especially valuable tool to assess potential risk and danger. Seeing these auras over time helped with her ability to understand and predict future events.

She had always experienced vivid dreams. When she met Chris and started developing her unique gifts her dreams became more significant in unusual ways. The vivid dreams and regular nightmares became ways of getting information and clues. The dreams terrified her, but she learned to stay with them as long as possible recognizing the importance of the information she received. Clues about current investigations, or remarkable events that sometimes could even predict the future. At times difficult to interpret she sometimes received information that was unclear, confusing, and might make sense days, weeks, months, and possibly even years later.

At a point when she was learning about her ability to see these auras, as well as other gifts she possessed, the auras began showing up in her dreams. It was the combination of two intense experiences. She would see a gray misty glow surrounding a person or entity in the dream. Jillian could sometimes feel an aura surrounding herself when involved in a dream. She would feel an intense temperature change and a color would develop showing like a veil or filter her eyes could see through. Everything in this view would appear altered by color and texture. The aura would be associated with strong emotion. Sometimes she would feel extreme fear, sadness, elation, and joy. Sometimes she would experience a horrible darkness she could not shake. A negative, endless void of hopelessness and isolation, and anger. Understanding her dreams was a work in progress and she did not always get it right. Her dreams were comprised of stories, images, and experiences with many dimensions and complexities.

Early on she learned spending time in places where high emotions are frequently experienced gave her the best opportunity to research and understand the auras. Prisons were ideal since she could talk with prisoners and research their histories. Hospitals were helpful, as well as psychiatric facilities. Nursing homes were especially helpful environments to research these auras. She found residents were cooperative, talkative, and appreciated the conversation.

She developed a color code that helped her to understand people and the auras surrounding them. She believed her color code to be often accurate although not perfect. Seeing a green aura represented peace and calm. A grey aura was a complex mix and could imply confusion, flux, and frantic transition. The chaos of a grey aura made it difficult for her to understand and interpret, however it did give her insight into the complexity of that person A blue aura typically showed detachment and disconnection from others. People with blue auras tended to negatively impact others. They often would remain in limbo with few true connections in life while living in solitude.

Red auras were often indicative of primitive and pervasive anger and negativity. A red aura could indicate a person with evil intentions, capable of anything, and potentially extremely dangerous. Red auras were rare, and Jillian had never really seen a purely red aura. She knew if she did ever see this it would indicate the potential for true evil in the worst sense of the concept.

These auras were rarely pure in color and to Jillian the combination of colors she would see represented every person's level of complexity. It was also proof to her that people can grow and shift showing certain personality traits that change over time. To her, this was always an optimistic and hopeful view of the human soul and spirit.

Jillian had to shift within herself to enable her to view these auras. If she was forced to see these colors surrounding people whom she encountered every day it would be overwhelmingly distracting. This information might also overly influence her throughout her daily encounters. She learned to control this ability and use it only when necessary. She did find it tempting sometimes to summon this information if she was looking to discern the true motivations behind a person's actions. Most of the time this was not necessary and using auras in this everyday way was in her opinion, unethical. Jillian tried only to obtain this information when it was most important, for the safety or well-being of others. Of course, she did not have control over seeing auras in her dreams. The colors felt forced upon her and added intensity and realism to her dreams that were almost unbearable at times.

In day-to-day life, she had the ability to control when she allowed herself to see these auras. Occasionally, however, her ability to control seeing these auras would be somehow disabled. On two occasions in the past, Jillian was forced to see these auras when awake and turning off this ability was not possible in the moment. These occasions were unique and rattled her to her core.

At the site of the accident, she stood on the road as the sun came up over the horizon. Mags sat next to her leaning on her leg and Jillian bent over to pat her head. Mags leaned into the pat on the head and licked her hand. Jillian felt deeply unsettled about what happened overnight. It was all starting to sink in and as she processed the night events it was as if a dark heavy blanket had been placed over her. It felt stifling and it took great effort to breathe.

Jillian and James continued to wait on the road next to their car as the sun could be seen brightly over the horizon. They talked quietly with one another while waiting for the police to interview them about the car accident and the interaction they had with the victims. Jillian started to tell James about the aura she saw around the man on the driver's side. "It was bright red, and I was forced to see it." James looked at her intently and said, "You mean like the aura you saw at the prison?" She shook her head yes. "I had the same feeling as I did that day in the prison. Something was forcing me to see the aura. It needed me to see it." "What concerns me most is the brilliant red color." James looked at her understanding what this meant. To Jillian, a bright or deep red aura meant inherent danger. A person who could be evil in nature. She had never seen a completely red aura around a person before. Being forced to see an aura was also an unsettling experience for her. A loss of control. An intrusion or invasion of her being. They both stood silently thinking about the implications of this experience.

When trying to understand the auras, Jillian spent time conducting research. It was during this research she had an unsettling experience. She was interviewing an inmate who was on death row for murder. She had chosen death row due to the serious crimes these convicts committed, and because these inmates were often cooperative, needing something to help them pass the time. When interviewing a particular inmate, she started seeing a reddish grey aura surrounding him. It was a large aura that was slowly absorbing this inmate as he was speaking. It turned into a brilliant red that surrounded him. She became immersed in viewing this aura to the point of not hearing what he was saying. She felt swept away within this red aura when she heard a voice speak to her. The voice said, "Why are you wasting time with this person when it's me you want to speak with?" She spoke out loud and asked, "What did you say?" The inmate repeated the sentence that was not the sentence she heard and not in the voice she heard speak it. She felt confused, when the voice spoke again, "Why are you wasting your time with this person when you should be speaking with me?" The second voice spoke over the inmate as he was talking about his family. The inmate's voice faded into the background as this louder more penetrating voice took over. Realizing something was terribly wrong Jillian jumped out of her chair and ran down the hall and out of the building. Something was trying to communicate with her through this inmate. It was forcing her to see this red aura and it felt evil. She sat in her car after this happened, trembling and sweating. She never returned to the prison again. This was a one-time experience or so she thought.

Back at the accident site James and Jillian were still waiting for the police. Standing at the car Jillian looked at James and said, "There is more. The driver in the car opened his eyes and spoke to me immediately before the car caught on fire. Before he started screaming." "The injured driver said in a strange, familiar, and terrifying voice," 'Why are you wasting your time with this person when you should be speaking with me?" "A moment later he also said in a different voice that seemed more appropriate to the person, "It is here. We made a mistake, and it is here." Jillian continued, "The second voice sounded scared and panicked. Then the fire broke out and the explosion happened." She took a breath and paused and asked James, "Did you hear him speaking?" James hesitated and said, "No I heard nothing." Jillian felt rattled since this was the same message she heard at the prison. She understood someone or something was trying desperately to communicate with her. It felt ominous and dark. Both the prisoner and the man in the car had the growing red auras. The second voice that sounded scared and panicked left her feeling sad. It was confusing and hard for her to sort out.

The police detective named Turner walked over to where they were standing and started asking questions. He reported it may take a while to identify the victims due to the fire. Jillian and James took turns giving their stories about what happened. They told the detective they had been camping and decided to hike back to the car when it started snowing. This explained why they were on the roads so late at night. Detective Turner told them he would call when the victims were identified. By this time, the tow truck had arrived to tow the car and take them to the nearest town.

They waited by the side of the road for the tow truck to arrive. When it arrived, the driver moved the damaged car onto the truck. When he finished, they all packed into the front cabin of the tow truck with Mags behind the passenger seat. The driver was a large man with a long, full beard. He seemed tired and Jillian assumed he had been awakened unexpectedly for this job. The driver remained quiet as he drove down the winding mountain roads to town. Jillian and James were exhausted and looked forward to finding a room in town to rest for a while. James had his arm placed behind the seat petting Mags. He quickly jumped and moved his arm as a white cat suddenly leaped onto Jillian's lap. She screamed and then laughed as she realized the cat was friendly. The cat kneaded Jillian's legs before settling in for a nap. Mags sat watching and wagging her tail. The tow truck driver said in a deep voice, that is my cat, Jocelyn. She likes riding in the truck. James laughed as he looked at Mags sitting in the back seat like nothing ever happened. Jillian said, "Mags has always liked cats."

Jillian and James decided to stay in town while a local mechanic evaluated the car. They hoped it could be repaired. They went to the town diner, a local family-owned restaurant, and ordered breakfast. The town of Susurrous Pines was small with one main street. The restaurant had photos of locals and a bulletin board with the community -based announcements. They drank coffee and ate; both absorbed in thought and exhausted after such a long night. Jillian felt the darkness and the finality of the two men who died in the accident. The significance of being the last people to ever hear those men speak. The importance of being the recipients of their final words before they died. The questions about how they ended up on the side of that cliff and the fate or coincidence that led Jillian and James to find them after experiencing a car accident so close by.

Jillian said, "We should call Chris and Bella and tell them what happened. They may be worried." James agreed and they called together. Bella and Chris had been waiting to hear from them. Bella was genuinely concerned about the two close calls they had with the accidents. She was very relieved Jillian and James did not get hurt. Chris was intrigued about Jillian's experience and the connection with what took place with the inmate at the prison. He encouraged them to take time to return to the estate. They had earned a break.

While at the restaurant they received the call about the car. It would take a few days to repair. The mechanic had to wait for parts and rebuild the front end. He seemed enthusiastic about the challenge. Jillian remarked that if this happened at home it would take weeks to get the car back. There was no backlog of cars to work on in this small town and the mechanic was happy to have the business. They were given a loaner car to use while the car was being repaired.

They decided to walk around the town and started down the main street. The town named Susurrous Pines had seen better days. It was incredibly old with many vacant stores and abandoned storefronts. It had a sad, drab, and dingy feel to it. Like looking through a photo filter that muted all the colors into shades of grey and brown. They passed an old church that still was in operation with announcements about services on the front display. They passed the Sheriff's office with one police vehicle parked in front. It was a small building that shared space with the local social services center. They passed a local library and a small museum along with a grocery store and a feed and farm store. The streets were lined with tall, old, and looming pine trees. It took about fifteen minutes to walk on Main Street through the town of Susurrous Pines. They found themselves standing in front of the covered bridge leading out of the town. As they stood Jillian looked up the mountain and noticed a large old stately, southern-style mansion looking down on the town. She could see a long winding road leading up to the house. At the bottom of the road leading to the house was a faded wooden painted sign that read The Chateau.

Chapter Three

The Chateau

They walked up the narrow winding road along the mountain leading to the Chateau to inquire about a room. It was a historic manor house, with an imposing presence as it was positioned on the mountainside. Jillian looked up at the towering pines lining the driveway. She could smell the strong scent of pine. Closing her eyes, she listened to the sound of the wind blowing through the trees. It was a soft swishing, whirring, and whispering sound that she found peaceful. She tried to focus on the sound as they walked. She felt on edge and deeply troubled after the recent events. Mags was trotting happily, investigating every smell along the way. As they approached the house, they could see tall, thick, ornate concrete white columns in front. The house had a deep wrap-around porch with swings, sofas, and chairs that appeared to have been outside for many years based on the faded and worn appearance. It was surrounded by forests with large pine trees. They walked up the steep front porch stairs wearing bulky hiking boots creating a hollow thumping noise with each step.

Jillian and James stood in front of the formidable front doors. Jillian lifted the heavy knocker and dropped it, knocking on the door three times. The knocker produced a loud, cavernous bang that reverberated throughout the house. James looked down and noticed a wooden sign that said. "Vacancy, please check at the front desk." Pushing open the large heavy wooden doors they walked into the front hall and were instantly impressed by the large space with soaring ceilings and large windows. Jillian said, "Wow, this house is huge."

After the initial impression of the vast and impressive front room, they were overtaken by the smell of burnt toast and stale coffee. The walls were covered with faded floral wallpaper and the hardwood floors were partially covered with worn and threadbare space rugs hiding the warped wooden planks. The carpet was colorful at one time and those colors were now drab and coated with layers of dirt and stain creating different shades of brown. The floor was uneven and soft in places causing a slight sinking feeling with certain steps and the floor creaked and groaned as they went. Walking on the warped floor created an off-balance feeling and Jillian touched the wall as she walked to help steady herself. The lighting was poor with the use of small lamps and dingy, dark lamp shades. Many of the lampshades had vintage, beaded fringe hanging on the ends. Jillian looked at James and said, "I think at one time this place was probably very grand." James glanced at the ceiling and noticed an antique appearing crystal chandelier. The crystals were covered in dust and clearly had not been cleaned in years. The muted light shining from the chandelier was barely visible as it could not penetrate the years of dirt coating the crystal glass.

The Chateau had available rooms. The owner, an elderly woman with long grey hair wearing a brown and gray full-length skirt and home knitted dark brown cabled sweater, seemed surprised to have new business. Her voice was raspy with a deep tone. She spoke in short sentences taking noisy breaths in between. The woman seemed overwhelmed and unprepared to have guests however she was still welcoming. In her deep raspy voice, she apologized to Jillian and James for the state of the house. She mentioned it was very old and over recent years she had difficulty keeping up with repairs. James noticed the elderly woman; with the colors worn in the various shades of brown and gray she blended in nicely with the décor at the Chateau. Fortunately, the owner of the Chateau was fond of dogs and took an immediate liking to Mags. She slowly bent down to pat her on the head and enthusiastically gave permission for Mags to stay with Jillian and James. The woman made it clear she was making an exception to the no-pet policy usually in place.

They walked up the long grand staircase stepped up the creaky stairs and walked down the lengthy hall to the room and unpacked. The room was pleasant enough with exceptionally large windows and a king-sized heavy wood-posted bed. They both sat on the bed and talked about feeling fatigued and sleepy. The bed creaked as they moved. James said, "Does everything creak and groan in this house?" "Yes, including us!" Jillian responded. They both laughed at this and decided to try to sleep for a while. It felt good to laugh after the intensity of the past day. It was a few hours before dinner time and due to the shorter days, the sun was already low in the sky. Mags curled up in between them with her head on a pillow.

Jillian jolted awake and sat up. Mags was sitting in front of the bedroom door whining. She looked at James who was sleeping peacefully. It was already dark outside, and they had been asleep longer than planned. Jillian sat on the edge of the bed and watched Mags. She was still sitting next to the door and seemed attentively listening to something. Her ears were twitching, and she held her head low the way she does when focusing on something identified as important in her world. Then she heard it. A shuffling noise outside in the hallway. Jillian walked over to the door and listened. A loud shriek came from down the hall. Jillian jumped and instinctively backed away from the door. She looked over at James again and this time he was sitting up wide-eyed. "What was that sound?" He asked. She said, "It sounded like a young girl screaming." Now they were both standing in the middle of the room waiting and listening. They walked closer to the door and Jillian held the doorknob, while slowly turning it. She slowly opened the door gently, waiting in anticipation. They both walked into the hallway while Mags stayed inside the room peering around the corner watching them.

The hallway was dimly lit by wall sconces that cast shadows down the walls and onto the floor. The hallway took on a completely distinctive look and overall impression at night. It was a special kind of darkness that contributed to the imagination and ominous notions of dread. They walked away from the bedroom and down the hall slowly. They rounded the corner toward the main staircase and Jillian screamed as she bumped into the owner who was also rounding the corner. She seemed as startled as Jillian and in her raspy, breathy voice said, "What are you doing slinking around the hallway like this?" "You could scare an old woman to death!" After catching her breath Jillian said, "We heard something in the hallway a few minutes ago." "It sounded like a young girl screaming." The old woman said, "This is an old house, and it makes unusual noises at night." "I am sure it was nothing." Unconvinced, Jillian and James made the way back to the bedroom. The old woman continued down the hall and disappeared down a back staircase.

They closed the door behind them and sat down on the bed. Jillian said, "There is something very strange about that woman." "I feel creeped out by her, and I didn't feel that way earlier." James nodded in agreement and said, "Did you notice Mags did not run over and greet her like she did before?" "Mags seemed to pick up on something different also." As they talked, they heard a loud boom, and the power went off. It was completely dark except for a small amount of light coming through the window from the moon outside. "Great, this is not getting any better," James said. They both sat very still for a moment waiting to see if the power came back on.

James stood up and walked over to the window. Their eyes had adjusted a bit to the darkness, and both could see in the dark more clearly now. He stood and surveyed the mountainside. There was a forest in the distance on one side and grassy fields on the other. He could see down the mountain and into the town below. He said, "It looks like the power went out all over town." It is completely dark down there." "Why would that happen?" Jillian asked. "Why would the entire town lose power?"

They decided to leave the room to find answers. Mags followed closely as they closed and locked the bedroom door. It was completely quiet except for the sound of their feet padding quietly on the thin, worn carpet. The hallway was much darker now, and they could barely see as they stepped. They both turned on flashlights from their phones to light the way directly in front of them. James grabbed Jillian's hand and they continued close together. Rounding the corner near the main staircase the outline of an elderly woman could be seen at the top of the stairs. Jillian called out to her, but the woman did not answer. She started slowly walking down the stairs. To Jillian, it seemed as if she was almost gliding. She could see no difference in the woman's steps from one stair to another. The woman had long thick gray hair and was wearing a full-length red dress. The dress was blowing around as she floated down the stairs. Jillian and James walked faster to catch up and Jillian called out again. "Hey, excuse me!" "We need to talk to you!" The woman continued down the stairs, and it seemed impossible she could not hear Jillian calling out to her. They ran down after her and caught up to the woman in the main entrance hall. Jillian touched the woman's shoulder and she slowly turned toward her. Jillian screamed and backed away when she saw the woman's face. James yelled, "What the....?" The woman's long grey hair had become jet black, thicker, and wavy and blew away from her face as she turned toward them. Her face appeared younger but the skin was still wrinkled and grey with a shimmery tone to it. The skin was thin and the bones from her face were showing through giving her a skeletal appearance. Her eyelids were red and black, swollen, and puffy. Her round black eyes peeked through the puffy lids and were distorted, bulbous, and round. Her stare was blank and unrelenting. She did not speak but held them in her gaze. Mags stood cowering behind Jillian whining and crying. They felt unable to move, frozen with fear and shock. Jillian sensed an intense impending danger being in the presence of this woman. She felt evil breaking through with her stare. The power of the energy was emanating, and she felt herself getting drawn into this spirit's being. Every second they were standing in front of her she understood was an opportunity for this evil to take hold. The front door blew open and strong wind filled the entry hall. The image of the woman with the long flowing black hair began to dissipate in the breeze, slowly becoming fainter until she became wisps of smoke blowing away in the gusty wind. When she was gone, the wind and negative energy also dissipated, and the air was calm again.

It felt peaceful and quiet in the house. They both sat down hard on the staircase sweaty and out of breath. While they sat recovering, the power kicked on again with a loud popping noise.

They looked at one another and both spoke at once. They paused and laughed nervously. James said, "I believe we were just in the presence of true evil. The darkness I felt looking into her eyes." Jillian put her hand on his shoulder and said, "I am not sure what just happened or why she showed herself to us but there must be a reason." James said, "Maybe it was a warning." She looked at him and thought about this idea. "Why would this woman/spirit/presence be trying to warn them?" Jillian said, "I felt like she wanted to harm us. I wonder why she disappeared when she did?" James looked through the window and could see the sun starting to appear between the mountains.

James slowly stood up and walked over to the open front door and looked down into the valley. He could see the power was back on everywhere. The sun was emerging between the mountains. Mags stood next to him in the doorway with her nose pointed up smelling the outdoor air.

Jillian joined James in the doorway, and they stood quietly taking it all in. The sun was rising, and the morning light reflected beautifully with brilliant shades of gold, orange and red, over the snow on the trees and buildings down below as it emerged over the mountains. It was a lovely bright morning, and this made it hard to imagine the darkness they just experienced such a brief time ago. It seemed like a nightmare they had just awakened from. The house, the town, and the entire landscape looked cheerful and optimistic in the bright morning light.

Jillian said, "I believe we have found our area to investigate James." He looked at her and nodded in agreement. She said, "Everything that has happened since we left the forest during the snowstorm has been strange." "The car accident we encountered, this mysterious town of Susurrous Pines, the Chateau and our experiences here, and especially the spirit we saw of the woman with the flowing black hair." "Something is very wrong in this town." James turned to her and touched her face. "We will stay until we understand what is happening here. I also believe we may have found what we are looking for. There is a foreboding darkness I can feel all around us." Jillian shuddered as she stood in the doorway in the morning cold. The chill came from deep within her. The kind of chill that is not easily shaken off.

Chapter 4

Susurrous Pines

Jillian and James went back to the room to get ready for the day. They were wide awake at this point and felt renewed energy and excitement to investigate the town of Susurrous Pines. The plan was to learn more about the town by visiting the Susurrous Pines Museum, a small local library, and an antique store they passed on the walk the day before. Standing on the large front steps of the Chateau on such a bright morning felt invigorating. The view was lovely and should have been peaceful if not for the ominous and dark feeling Jillian carried with her. They stepped down the front stairs and began the walk down the winding road leading to the town. Mags walked next to them veering away occasionally to sniff something in the grass next to the road. She never strayed far. They stopped first at the diner to have breakfast. Mags walked into the diner with them and sat next to the table looking around with her nose in the air smelling the cooking food. It was the classic small-town diner with the booths lined along the windows and the fake leather seats in a shade of brown. The kitchen and eat-in bar were located in the center with the pivoting bar stools supported by the metal bases. The kitchen area in the back could be viewed through a large cutout window with a counter for placing orders when finished. Pastry displays sat on top of the counter as well as in a glass case near the cash register. It was clean but plain with little décor other than beige vinal upholstery. The lighting in the diner was bright using a combination of fluorescent lights in the ceiling and pedestal lights over the tables and bar area. The fluorescent lights buzzed softly and flickered erratically. In the background country music was playing. James said quietly, "Wow, I feel like we just stepped back in time. Maybe into the 1940s!" Jillian nodded her head, and they chose a table.

When seated, an older woman with an antique style apron edged with lace and a name tag on her chest that read Erin walked up to their table with a pot of coffee. She filled the cups and asked if they were ready to order. The menu was small and offered a handful of basic entree choices.

While eating they received a call from Chris. Chris asked Bella to join the call while Jillian and James detailed the events from the night before. Chris and Bella were staying at the estate hours away by car waiting to hear from them to determine the paranormal research investigation group's next research venture. The previous investigation they had named the Edin house investigation, lasted months and required recovery time when it was over. The team ultimately found themselves in a fight with true evil. The magnitude of the challenge experienced during the Edin house investigation was much more than anyone had anticipated. It was an experience they would never forget. The team understood it was just a matter of time before evil broke through again, and it was necessary to identify the place where this was most likely to happen.

Jillian and James had volunteered to investigate the forests in the mountains above the Susurrous Pines town to see if the rumors panned out. The forests written about in articles detailing strange occurrences, visions, shadow figures, and disappearances dating back centuries. The stories were remarkably similar to the recent research investigation that pushed them to the brink and challenged everything they knew and understood about this world. The discovery of other hidden realms that exist along with ours and contain dark spirits forever trying to break through and contaminate our world by spreading their virus.

They never had a real opportunity to find out more about the forest surrounding Susurrous Pines since the snowstorm forced a premature end to the research. Jillian and James believed it is perhaps the town and the surrounding area that could be the source of the problem and the danger. The feelings of joy and success following the previous Edin house investigation were short-lived. Soon after, they found out about the mysterious happenings in the forests near the town of Susurrous Pines.

So much had happened over the past six months. Chris discovered Jillian and James and identified them as integrals. They learned about their origins and special abilities and discovered the important responsibilities that go along with being an integral. Protecting the world against the evil always working to break through and destroy life as we all know it. Learning of their importance was still a bit surreal to both Jillian and James. Jillian, James, and the team faced new purpose, new dangers, and new commitments as significant working components of Nature's Integral Spirit. They were a part of this legacy now and intended to live the mission, working in secrecy.

After talking with Chris and Bella a plan was created to bring the team to Susurrous Pines to complete thorough research and investigation of the area. Jillian and James would spend time exploring to see if they could find any clues before the team assembled. In the past, the team would not usually research a potential site before the first investigation night due to concerns about contamination. Learning too much information about a site could potentially influence the findings. They decided to change this policy after the Edin house investigation. So much happened and the research was necessary to prepare them for the danger they encountered. They would not have survived without the important preparations and planning based on the research. Now the plan was to find out as much information as possible before and during the investigation.

Jillian and James were the only customers in the diner. There was the cook in the back and the server. The server tried to look busy behind the bar area while they ate. Jillian said, "This is very strange." "Where are all of the people?" James looked around and glanced outside. There were no cars driving on the main street. He looked at her and said, "It is very strange." "Almost like a ghost town."

They finished eating and walked out to survey the town. A block down was a museum, and this is where they decided to start. The museum was located within an old house that was operating as an antique store. One of the first houses built in the town from the look of it. It was an aged, gray wooden house sitting close to the sidewalk and road. The front porch was only two steps above the ground level. The house had low ceilings and plank floors with large gaps between the planks. Standing in the doorway, they looked at displays positioned all around the perimeter of the large front room. The displays showed old photos with descriptions. The displays were numbered, and Jillian stopped at the first and viewed the photo while reading the description. It was a black and white photo of men wearing dusty clothes and hats carrying equipment on their backs and in satchels. The description talked about Susurrous Pines being established as a gold mining town. The town boomed and experienced rapid growth during its heyday.

As they walked slowly through the displays the story of the town unfolded. It played out as so many gold rush and mining towns did. Initial success and prosperity that led to greed, excessive alcohol and drug use, gambling, violence, crime, prostitution, murder, and overall unrest. The separation between the wealthy families and the poor families became more divided. The workers in the mines became frustrated with earning low pay while the mine owners became wealthy and prospered. The living conditions for most deteriorated over time. Opportunity was limited and the locals began to leave. By the 1980s, the town was a shell of its former self with just a handful of the anchor families still living there. The old mines remained and were still located on the mountainsides surrounding the town.

The old photos captivated Jillian. She felt transfixed looking closely at all the people who lived in the town so long ago. Aged black and white staged photos of families sitting on their front porches or standing in front of homes. The somber looks on their faces. Even the children rarely smiled in these old photos. She remembered reading that the older photography technology required people to stay still for extended periods of time to prevent the photos from coming out blurry. It was easier for people to stay still for extended periods of time without holding a smile. Regardless of the reason, she always felt these photos made people look incredibly somber and unhappy. Perhaps also an indication of the challenging times they lived in.

It all felt strangely familiar although she could not explain why. James was over at a different display standing motionless. She walked over to see what he was looking at. He said, "Look closely at these photos." She looked closely and recognized the Chateau. It looked beautiful in these older photos sitting large on the hill. It was the story of the Chateau and the original family who built it. As she was standing with James viewing the photos an older man walked up behind them. He said, "We don't get many visitors here these days." "Where are you from?" Jillian jumped at the sound of his voice thinking they were alone. She turned around and found herself looking at a stately appearing man with gray hair and glasses. He was dressed formally in a fancy shirt and tie although the fashion was very outdated and strange to her. He had a kind face and seemed sincere about his interest in them.

James explained they were visiting while the car was repaired. The man carefully studied them with red, bloodshot eyes and then looked at the display they were viewing. James, with his back to the man as he viewed the museum display, stated they were staying at the Chateau. The man shifted back and forth on his feet nervously and said, "We don't get many visitors here these days." Jillian thought it was odd he repeated the same sentence and turned around to speak with the man. He was not there. She quickly glanced around the room to catch a glimpse of him, and he was nowhere to be found. She grabbed his arm and said, "James, the man is not here anymore." James turned from looking at the display and scanned all around the room. He asked, "Where could he have gone so quickly?" She said, "It's like he just disappeared." I would have seen him walking away." Jillian could feel her heart beating faster. James felt a chill down his spine. They both looked at one another knowingly. The people in this town seemed very odd. There was something very unusual about this town.

They both temporarily shrugged off the strange experience and turned back to the display about the Chateau. It was built by a wealthy businessperson for his family when the town was first settled. He invested in gold prospecting after it had been discovered in the hills surrounding the town. Then Jillian read something that chilled her to the core. She gasped and James looked over as he watched her face turn pale with beads of sweat on her forehead. He said, "What is it?" "What is wrong?" She said, "James read this section." She pointed to a section of the display. He read the section and stood motionless. A member of the Luster family built The Chateau. Jillian asked, "Could it just be a coincidence?" She went on, "Given everything we have experienced and been guided toward over recent months I cannot imagine this is a coincidence." James said. This must be an important connection to help us understand what happened during the Edin house investigation. There are connections to the Edin house and Susurrous Pines. They both stood in deep thought contemplating the possible meaning of this latest information.

Jillian took a breath and said, "Let's keep going through the displays." As they walked on, they learned about the Native American populations that originally lived in the Susurrous Pines area. Authentic Native American clothing was on display, as well as tools, weapons, and dream catchers. James stopped as they stood in front of the dream catchers. Jillian looked at him and asked, "Should you try?"

Dream catchers were the first items James touched as he was learning about his abilities. Dream catchers catch dreams and strong emotions and tend to leave intense imprints making it easier for him to absorb information. He paused and said, "Yes let's do it." He stood firmly with both feet solidly on the floor. He took a breath and reached out to hold the first dream catcher. Jillian held on to the table for balance. A wind developed around James as he held the dream catcher. The wind became stronger whirling around him. Jillian decided it would be easier to sit on the floor and stay low. She watched in amazement as James was surrounded by the wind and energy he created. She understood why this process was so exhausting for him. James heard the ringing in his ears and the rush of wind moving around him. The ringing became louder and the pounding in his head became more forceful. Then the rush of information. A flood of information and fragmented stories. He let go of the dream catcher and fell to the floor catching his breath. Jillian scooted over on the floor to sit next to him. She gently placed her hand on his shoulder and gave him a light hug.

James sat on the floor collecting himself and started to describe what he saw and felt. "There was a lot of unrest after the town was settled." "The Native Americans were concerned about the destruction of the land from the gold mining. They believed the settlers did not respect the land." He continued, "I saw fragmented dreams that showed fear and worry. Strong emotions and feelings of desperation. I also saw fighting. The Native Americans were fighting for the sacred land they felt was being destroyed. The dream catcher was filled with anger, pain, and grief. After a while, there was a darkness that infiltrated. Many nightmares involving evil monsters and dark spirits. The final image I saw was desolation. It was the landscape surrounding Susurrous Pines, but it looked wiped out. The landscape was brown and dead with nothing left living. The final image was more like a warning, or a premonition." Jillian said with a concerned look "Wow, that is very dark and full of impending doom." He closed his eyes and rested for a few minutes.

As was typical when James used this ability the information was in pieces. The rush of images and emotions did not always contain enough to complete a story and the information was often missing important parts. Jillian understood that James needed time to process the images he received. He would sometimes circle back to the discussion adding details or to fit the pieces together like a puzzle. They sat together quietly and when he was ready, they continued to walk through the museum displays. The remaining tour focused on the building architecture in the town and provided more information about the influential residents and their achievements. They did not learn any additional new information that could be helpful to them for the investigation.

After the museum tour was completed, they stood outside on the sidewalk in the sun. James was holding a map of the town. It was cold and sunny, and the fresh air felt good. Jillian suggested they do a walking tour of the residential areas. They chose to walk to the left down the main street first. They turned onto a side street and walked along a tree-lined road with stately homes on each side. Most homes were abandoned and dilapidated, however, occasionally they would come across a home that was in good condition with current residents. The well-kept homes were standouts among the crumbling neglected homes. Jillian wondered why people would want to live in a neighborhood with mostly abandoned and condemned houses. The large homes reminded them of the Chateau. At one time they were grand, and this neighborhood was sought after as a place of prestige requiring money and success to live there. It was a small neighborhood with just a few streets. They continued the walk and noticed changes in the scenery. The homes became smaller and smaller as they walked until they came to a larger neighborhood with one to two-room homes. The homes looked very much the same, and James called them cookie-cutter houses. They were located close to the street with small driveways. All these homes were abandoned and in a terrible state of deterioration. Most of the homes had aged signs on the front doors stating they were condemned. Jillian and James walked by rusted-out playgrounds, school buildings, ancient and decrepit-looking churches and places of worship, and an old community center with what was left of an outdoor pool.

The next neighborhood they entered was lined with aged tenement buildings. These buildings were also deteriorating and collapsing. There were crumbling stores located between the tenement buildings. It was an incredibly sad and depressed part of town. They continued to walk and found themselves back on the main street about a mile down on the other side from where the Chateau was located. Jillian suggested they walk to the antique store next.

The antique store was located in a historic house in a prime spot on Maine street. The house had a low wrap-around front porch that sat close to street level. Stately columns stood out front and the wood plank house looked a faded shade of dark blue. The color appeared bleached out in areas from long-term sun exposure. It had first-floor-level windows as well as two upper dormer windows and a small single front door painted black. The house had pretty features including custom carved shutters with decorative edges and a stained-glass window depicting a mountain landscape above the door.

The business had placed certain antique items out on the porch for display. James and Jillian stepped onto the front porch and walked around to look at the items. There was a life-size wooden sculpture of a bear standing next to the door with a plaque that had the local artist's name, and the date it was created- 82 years ago.

They noticed an antique weaving loom and a wooden rocking chair with a vintage doll sitting in it along with three collectible teddy bears. A small shelf held vintage bottles in various shapes and sizes in green, clear, and blue colored glass. The sign above the front door read 'Susurrous Pines Antiques'. Jillian opened the door, and it made a jingling noise from the chimes hanging above it as they walked through. The door closed with a thud as the wind chimes slowed and the sound stopped.

They stood in a smallish room. The items for sale were organized by categories. A section with lamps, a section with vintage tableware, one area with blankets and throws, and a four-poster bed covered with antique dolls.

James walked into an adjoining room and Jillian followed. She said, "This room has a very different feel to it." It was an interior room with no windows and poor lighting. It was filled with items related to the Christian religion. Antique crosses of many sizes, altars and ceremonial tables, rows of pews, stained glass hanging on the wall depicting various religious scenes, and a bookcase with rows of old bibles.

They continued into another room. This third interior room was very dimly lit. James noticed a bookcase with books on subjects related to witchcraft. A long table covered with different candles intended for use in various rituals, spells, and other practices. There was a cabinet displaying different sage bundles for burning. Another large table was stacked with various spirit boards. Certain spirit boards were in the original packaging while other boards were stacked without the additional pieces. A portable, collapsible wooden pentagram was propped up next to one of the tables. Around the perimeter of the room, different dark-colored fabrics were loosely hanging and draped. These fabrics were even hanging from the ceiling in the corners. Jillian jumped when she noticed a stone gargoyle on a pedestal in one of the corners. The hanging fabric with the low lighting created many unusual shadows in the room. The shadow created by the gargoyle was quite monstrous. James laughed after seeing her reaction. She scoffed, "It is not funny. That gargoyle is creepy and startled me!" James decided not to tease her too much about this one. He walked up to her and placed his arm around her. She said, "I feel very uneasy in this room. It has a very macabre and dark atmosphere. Let's leave now."

As they turned around to leave, a little girl walked into the room. She was about six years old, very thin, and pale with large brown eyes. She had curled brown hair in two ponytails tied off with pink ribbons to match a long pink dress. She looked at Jillian and James with her large brown eyes and asked in a small voice, "Are you interested in buying something? I can get my mom if you need help." Jillian answered, "We would like to speak to your mom if she is free." James looked at Jillian inquisitively, wondering what she was up to. The little girl turned around and left the room. Jillian looked at James and said, "I would like to meet the owner of this store and ask her a few questions." They waited around for about ten minutes and when the little girl's mother did not show up, they decided to walk around the store one more time before giving up on speaking with the owner.

Taking a lap around the entire store they did not see anyone else in the building. Jillian walked toward the front door. She said, "This town is so quiet. We have just seen a handful of people."

James and Jillian continued walking down the sidewalk to a nearby park to discuss the day. They did not have time to visit the library, however, the visit to the museum and the walking tour of the town, and even the antique store yielded interesting and helpful results. The library would be visited at another time.

Jillian said, "Let's go over what we have learned so far." "Susurrous Pines was first settled as a gold mining town." The Luster family started the town by building the Chateau and the first town buildings." "The Native Americans were very upset about the use of their land and small battles broke out." "The town eventually won and took over the Native American land."

James said, "The town thrived in the beginning years developing a booming gold industry centered around the Luster family who benefited the most financially from all of the dealings." "People from all over the country were drawn to this town by the hope and possibility of hitting it rich through prospecting gold." "The American dream." Jillian said, "Unfortunately the Luster family kept tight grips on all of the opportunity and most of the profits and left the workers to live in poverty chained to the town." "Families lived in poverty-stricken areas of town and drinking, gambling, prostitution, and crime ran rampant." "Murders were common, and anger grew towards the Luster family over time." "Families resorted to enlisting children to work in the mines. The mines were dangerous and often deadly places." James continued, "Eventually families and residents were forced to pick up everything and leave as it became too dangerous and difficult to exist in the town."

Jillian said, "A town built on greed that eventually died out through pain, strife, and sorrow." "That sounds like a potential breeding ground for evil." James nodded in solemn agreement. He said, "The name Susurrous Pines came from the Native American belief that when the wind blows through the pine trees they are whispering." "The trees whispering in the wind sharing the secrets of the forest."

Chapter 5

Dangerous Dreams

They were beginning to feel very tired from the two previous nights. Jillian said, "I could really use some sleep." James asked, "Should we return to the Chateau during daylight hours and try to sleep for a while? Chris, Bella, and the rest of the team should arrive in the late evening. It's early enough now so we can sleep for a couple of hours and then continue our research in the town." Jillian answered, "I think we should be safe to go back to the Chateau during the day, but I do not want to go back by ourselves at night again." James nodded in agreement, and they started the walk back to the Chateau. Mags was happily trotting next to them looking up at their faces occasionally, hoping for a pat on the head.

They turned down the long road leading to the Chateau. The ground was still solid from the recent freezing weather. James listened to the crunching sound of the pine needles under their feet as they stepped. Jillian looked up, watching the large tree branches swaying in the wind. She picked up a stick and threw it for Mags to chase. Mags happily brought it back and dropped the stick at her feet and she threw it again. This continued until Mags became tired and she dropped the stick to walk between Jillian and James again. When they arrived at the Chateau, the old woman was standing in the front hallway wearing the same full-length skirt and home knitted cable sweater. She appeared a bit confused standing in the hall with a look on her face like she was trying to remember her immediate direction and purpose. The woman jumped as she was startled when Jillian and James walked through the front door and took her by surprise. Mags ran up to her and she slowly bent down to pet her. She asked if they slept well last night. Jillian looked at James and she answered, "We have had better nights." The woman looked at her and said, "Yes, the house can make a lot of unusual noises if you are not used to it." "It comes alive at night." She followed up by saying, "I haven't slept well in years but maybe that's what happens when you get old." She turned and walked slowly down the big hall toward the dining and kitchen area.

They walked up the front staircase and turned the corner toward their room. This time as they were walking by the rooms in the hallway Jillian noticed above one of the doors a plaque that read "William's Room". Could that be William Luster she wondered? They arrived at their room and closed and locked the door. Mags jumped on the bed and within minutes they were all sleeping soundly.

Jillian was awakened by a sound outside the door. It was a scraping and scratching noise. Mags was sitting on alert at the edge of the bed. James was sleeping and instead of waking him, she decided to investigate on her own.

She walked over following the source of the scraping sound. Mags followed and suddenly they jumped as something shot out from under the door and then retracted quickly. Then once again, a shadow pushed through the gap between the door and the floor and retracted quickly. At first, shocked Jillian relaxed after realizing there was a cat outside the door. He was reaching under the door with his paw and then pulling it back. She heard a meow as the cat batted its paw around under the door. Mags stayed at attention watching the paw carefully as it moved around under the door. Jillian breathed a sigh of relief and smiled.

She turned to walk back to the bed when she heard something much larger moving in the hallway. The cat heard it also and let out a screech before taking off and running down the hall. Loud shuffling and banging noises were coming from down the hall. The sounds were getting louder and seemed closer. She could not identify the source of the sounds but understood something large was making noise in the hallway. The ominous feeling of dread began to take over as the hairs on the back of her neck and arms stood up and she felt goosebumps all over her body. She looked over at James and said, "James wake up." 'James!" Mags stayed at attention moving her ears around and listening to the noises. The bumping, shuffling and banging became louder as whatever was out in the hall moved closer to the door. Jillian and Mags remained still as they stood close to the door. When the footsteps sounded like they were right next to the door they abruptly stopped. Jillian could hear her heart beating and felt her shallow breaths. Then she heard breathing outside the door. Loud, long raspy breaths just on the other side. She quickly checked back and noticed James still sleeping. Looking under the door she could see a shadow moving back and forth. The breathing continued and seemed to be getting louder. Then the doorknob started to rattle. Whatever was outside the door was trying to get in. Mags whined and moved backward toward the bed and away from the door. Jillian grabbed the doorknob and tried to prevent it from turning. She could feel the force coming from the other side. She held it tightly with both hands preventing it from moving. The breathing outside the door continued and became louder and even raspier. She could feel drops of cold sweat flowing down her face. She looked over at James again wondering why he was not waking up. She yelled his name with no response. She was torn between holding the doorknob and running to check on James. She felt completely panicked and did not understand why James was not waking up. She let go of the doorknob and ran to the bedside. She shook him and he did not move or wake up. She could see he was breathing. The sheet was pulled up over his head and she lifted it to look at his face. She jumped back when she saw the person in the bed was not James. The figure in the bed was ghoulish looking with grey shriveled skin and wisps of white hair. It had shrunken bulbous deep-set eyes and thin lips revealing sharp yellowed teeth. The eyes were bright red and glowing. It had the pure red aura surrounding it. The aura was growing and looked like liquid dripping around and off the creature, leaving pools of red liquid on the bed. She felt desperate as if it would engulf her and she would disappear forever. Jillian felt the cold wetness on her body. She had freezing cold red liquid dripping from her forehead, and her arms. She screamed a shrieking scream while backing away. The creature emitted a horrible, putrid smell that combined the scent of dead animal with sewer or sulfur. The smell burned her eyes and hurt her lungs as she frantically gasped for breath. The figure sat up slowly while watching her with unblinking red sunken eyes. Jillian could hear Mags whining somewhere in a dark corner of the room. She could see the red aura surrounding this being. The brilliant red aura that was dripping red liquid all around it leaving puddles on the floor and splattering the slimy substance all over the ceiling and walls. She turned to run out of the room when she felt it. A hard, unforgiving hand grabbing her shoulder. The creature violently pulled her back toward the bed, and she felt a searing pain moving from her shoulder down her back. Long bony fingers slicing into the skin on her shoulder. She could feel the fingers and long nails breaching her skin and entering her body. The creature laughed a deep, slow, raspy laugh that vibrated within her body. There was intense pain and the sensation of bony fingers moving around within her shoulder displacing her skin, blood, and sinews. She felt her own warm blood running down her back. Jillian cried, screamed, and tried to run. She felt the bottom drop out and fell to the floor.

He was gently shaking her. "Jillian wake up." "Wake up!" She slowly opened her eyes and when her eyes came into focus, she saw James kneeling next to the bed with his arms around her. He said, "You were having a terrible nightmare and I couldn't wake you up." She was sweating, breathing hard, and could feel her heartbeat in her throat. The dream seemed so real. It was still light out at about 3:00 in the afternoon. They had been sleeping for hours. James looked intense as he helped her sit up. She said, "It was so real." "My dreams are becoming even more intense. There is something about this place, it is powerful." She started to remember the figure in the bed and the hand penetrating her shoulder. She moved her hand to touch around her shoulder and winced in pain. Her hand was covered in blood. She sat up and looked behind her. Blood covered the pillow and the sheets. Her shoulder was throbbing, and James said, "Oh my god what happened?"

He ran to get a towel and applied it to the deep wound on her shoulder. She jumped when he placed it on the wound. "We need to get this cleaned up." "They must have a first aid kit at the front desk." She started to tell him about her dream. She gave him the details as he worked to stop the bleeding. He was very disturbed by this new intensity to her dreams. She had never actually been seriously harmed during a nightmare and this was a game-changer. A new level of worry. "How can a person be protected from their dreams?" James thought to himself.

They walked down the front staircase and over to the front desk. The old woman did not seem to be around. Jillian said, "Maybe we can look around in the office area for a first aid kit or bandages." They walked down the back hall to the office area. They looked around on the shelves and around the desk and Jillian saw a bathroom off from the nearby hall. She went in and found a small container of old bandages on the shelf. She took it and they started walking back to the hall. They both looked around and James said, "look at all of the dust and dirt." "It looks like this area has not been cleaned in years." The back-office area had an old musty smell, much more noticeable compared to other rooms in the house.

They sat on the front porch and James cleaned the wound and put a bandage on it. Jillian was feeling better, and she tried not to think about the severity of what happened. She said, "James this dream meant something." "This dark figure, this creature that attacked me in our room was sending us a dire message. It was a warning. If we stay and investigate Susurrous Pines, we are placing ourselves and the team in danger. We need to make sure everyone understands what we might be getting ourselves into." James said, "Everyone on the team understands the innate danger in what we do. Our mission will always carry with it great personal risk. We will share with them everything we have learned so far, as well as our gut feelings and intuition. We will all be afraid- it comes with the territory." They both sat and thought about everything they had learned and what they had experienced since they had been in Susurrous Pines including; the car accident, the second car accident with the two men and the car fire, the Chateau and the strange old woman who runs it, the woman with the black flowing hair, the strange old man in the museum, the town's founding family named Luster and the possible connection to William Luster and the previous Edin house investigation, the Native American local tribes and the pain and violence they experienced related to the land and the takeover by the settlers and gold miners, the greed, violence, poverty and downward spiral the town experienced, the ultimate desperation of the town's people leading to the eventual near desertion of the town, Jillian's recent intense nightmare with the ghoulish figure and the shoulder wound. Going over these facts, supported the belief that the town of Susurrous Pines is a hot spot for paranormal and supernatural activity. They both felt a powerful dark presence in the town and surrounding areas. They sat on the front porch and waited for the team to arrive.

Jillian and James joined the Paranormal Spirit Research and Investigations Team and met Chris while learning to develop their special abilities. They learned about their identities as Integrals, and the significant role they are to play in the fight between good and evil. An ancient fight that has taken place since the beginning of time. Chris is part of a family that through the ages inherited the responsibility of finding the integrals within each generation. Responsible for finding a needle in a haystack. Chris became the financial donor of the Paranormal Spirit Research and Investigations Team with the hope that integrals would be attracted to such groups. People with very special gifts and abilities that would eventually show during research investigations with heightened emotions and fear. He spent years searching all the time knowing failure was not an option. The end of the world, Armageddon, it has been called many things. The end of life as we know it. The beginning of something so dark and unimaginable it was difficult to even conceptualize. Chris's ancestors had written in detail about what could take place if the world balance is not maintained. It was a heavy burden for Chris to carry and one he was born into. He was raised to continue this work as his life's purpose.

The Paranormal Investigations Team was on the way, and they would need to develop a plan when they arrived.

Chapter 6

Uncovering Clues and Meeting the Team

The Paranormal Spirit Research and Investigations Team is science-based and approaches all research with skepticism. The team members became interested in the paranormal after having a momentous experience of their own that could not be explained.

Chris is the financial donor and oversees the investigations. He participates when needed and takes a guiding role in assisting Jillian and James, with the use and development of their abilities.

Matt is the group leader and founder. He had a chilling experience as a young child that to this day he has not spoken about with the group.

Angie is the tech specialist. She stays on top of the latest technology and gear and leads the tech setup for each investigation. She shared a haunting experience with her sister when they were young and on a family vacation at a lake house. Angie continues to search for answers and plans to return to that same lake house one day to investigate.

Nick helps with the video coverage during an investigation. Team members review the tapes and then he edits the film coverage to focus on any findings. He is quick to be skeptical and often provides comic relief. He had an experience as a child when visiting his grandparents. He could not explain what he saw. This experience never left him, and he joined the team with the hope of finding answers.

Aden is the risk-taker of the group and often volunteers for the most challenging jobs during an investigation. He too wants to find answers to the experiences he had growing up. He was tortured by constant sleepwalking, sleep disruption, and nightmares as a child. During previous investigations, Aden was found to have a special vulnerability and sometimes made a special connection with the dark spirits they encounter. This connection and vulnerability allowed the spirits to inhabit his body for periods of time. He would never have any memory of these invasions although other team members observed these events. These experiences left an impact on him personally and he struggles with the risk the investigations might pose for him. During the previous Edin house investigation, Aden needed assistance from Jillian and James to escape from the dark spirits on several occasions. He is brave but will back off if it becomes clear an encounter or situation during an investigation might pose a special threat to him.

Jillian started out as the primary researcher for the investigations. She would research details of the locations and report her findings to the team. Since discovering her gifts Jillian's role has become more significant and she is seen as another leader along with James and Matt. Her ability to obtain clues and information from her vivid dreams, the ability to see auras, her unique intuition, as well as her ability to receive communications from spirits have proven to be priceless to the investigations. She helps to guide the direction of the investigations and research as well as intervenes and works with James when needed to fight back the dark spirits and evil. Jillian and James discovered they can use their special abilities together and the joining of energies creates more power to defend against evil.

James was added to the team after discovering his gifts and the combined strength when working with Jillian. His ability to absorb information from objects as well as create the energy force along with Jillian to fight back the dark spirits and evil when needed proved to be extremely valuable.

Chris's cousin Bella was also added to the team after discovering her special ability to keep one foot in this world and one foot within the spirit world for brief periods of time. She could temporarily break through the barrier to discover essential information and provide unique insights into the spirit world. The rare use of her abilities has created a connection to the dark spirit dimension that forever haunts her and becomes more invasive each time. She cannot completely sever the connection she created beyond the barrier. Each experience leaves an imprint that stays with her. These risks make her participation in investigations extraordinarily dangerous. For this reason, her abilities are used only when absolutely necessary, and for the shortest lengths of time. She has saved team members on many occasions and volunteers to take this risk believing the gift was given to her for a reason.

Jillian and James talked quietly while sitting on the front steps of the Chateau. The team was scheduled to arrive any minute. Mags was happy sitting on the highest step surveying the landscape and keeping watch. The wind was picking up and they could hear it whirring through the pines. Mags raised her nose, closed her eyes, and sniffed the air. Jillian pulled her heavy coat higher up on her neck as the wind became stronger. James said, "Look, here they come!" A caravan of three cars turned to drive up the long winding road leading to the Chateau. Bella and Chris drove together, Matt and Angie drove the team van and Nick and Aden drove together in Nick's car. They watched the caravan make its way up the hills and around the curves. Jillian and James waved as they drove up and parked.

Bella and Chris were the first to walk up the steps to greet them followed by the rest of the team. Mags had to greet everyone individually and after the initial greetings were finished, she started over with Chris and Bella again. They were happy to oblige, and Bella knelt to greet Mags face to face. Mags nuzzled her hands and face and gave her a big wet lick. Bella proceeded to laugh and wiped her face with a sleeve. After the initial warm greetings, they all sat together to talk. Jillian and James filled them in on the experiences so far, along with everything they learned from the research. It was a lot of information, and the team was glued to every detail asking questions along the way. There was a lot of excitement after they were finished. Everyone could feel the potential for an active investigation. They had never investigated a whole town and the surrounding area before. Jillian was surprised at her reaction to the team's arrival. She was incredibly happy to see them and felt a huge relief at the site of the caravan driving up. There was more safety in numbers she felt. They had experience working together as a team and she sincerely trusted each team member.

James suggested they check in to the Chateau and then they could all go to the diner and eat while they plan the next steps. The group walked into the front hall and looked around. The old woman came to meet them and gave them room keys. The team would all be staying in the same wing at the top of the main staircase and down the hall to the left. They settled in and then met in the front hall. The group readied themselves to walk down the hill and into the town.

There was a lot of excited chatter as they walked. Matt said, he found the Chateau remarkably interesting. He could feel a strange energy there. He also found the old woman who ran the place very unusual. Something about her was off. They all agreed but could not pin down what concerned them. Jillian spoke about how the woman wandered around the halls and the staircases at all hours of the night.

They arrived at the diner, walked in, and sat in a large booth next to the window. They were the only customers and the only people in the building other than the server and the cook. Aden commented about how quiet the town was. Nick looked around and shivered from a chill. Angie thought the town was charming and it looked like it had been very grand at one time. "I love the old structures and the big pine trees," Angie said. Nick felt troubled by what he saw. He felt very uneasy and uncomfortable ever since they crossed through the covered bridge into the town. He was not sure why and stated so when he told the group, "I am not sure but something about this whole town feels very wrong. Maybe it's the history and what has happened here over the years. Maybe those dark events have left residual energy." "Whatever it is I think we need to tread very carefully." James chose this moment to show the group what happened to

Jillian's shoulder. She pulled up the back of her shirt and lifted the bandage. Jillian shuddered in pain as James gently pulled the bandage up. The group gasped when they saw the deep wound. Angie asked, "Are you ok?" Jillian nodded her head and said she just wanted to move on from it. Matt said, "We need to be very careful during this investigation." "Maybe we shouldn't split up as much as we normally would to cover such a large area." "Maybe we need to stick together even if it takes more days to complete." They all agreed with this idea.

Dinner was loud and boisterous as the group talked and planned. As they discussed and ate, Jillian glanced over at the bulletin board. It was covered with paper stuck on with tacks. She stood up and walked over to take a look. There was a flyer about a missing dog and a faded photo. Another advertisement for tutoring high school math. A paper offering babysitting services with the phone number torn off a few times at the bottom. Then Jillian froze. Her eyes landed on a newspaper clipping about funeral services with a picture. The picture was of an elderly man wearing old-fashioned but elegant clothes. She stared at the yellowed and faded newspaper clipping. She stepped closer to study the face of the man in the picture recognizing it was the man they encountered at the museum. The man's name was Flannery Token and he died in 1955. She gasped and started to read the obituary. He ran the museum as well as a local bar for half of his life and was born in Susurrous Pines. She stood staring trying to understand the implications of this.

The woman who was working at the diner as their server walked over to her. Jillian felt her presence from behind and turned around to speak to her. "This man, I have seen him in town." "We saw him in the museum." The woman said, "He died a long time ago and was loved around here." "We keep his photo on the bulletin board because he likes it there." "He was very attached to this town." Jillian looked at her and said, "How do you know he likes his picture there?" The woman answered in a very matter-of-fact way, "He has told me many times." Jillian looked at her oddly. It was the first time she really focused on this woman's face and her features. She was between about 60 to 70 years old with long black hair mixed with gray. She had dark eyes and looked as though she spent a lot of time in the sun over the years. She had deep wrinkles and worry lines on her forehead, and around her mouth. She turned around to grab the coffee pot and refill the cups at the table. Jillian stayed in place looking intently at the bulletin board. As she studied the other postings, she realized they were all older posts. Yellowed, crumpled paper, older copy paper that had the bluish ink and poor ink quality. Why would they keep such old posts on the wall? It was very creepy to think that Flannery Token was speaking to the woman at the diner. How eerie it was that they met him at the museum knowing he died so many years ago.

Jillian walked over to the table and said, "James, I need you to see something over here." He walked over with her, and she showed him the obituary with the photo of Flannery Token. He read it and looked at her. He studied it again and said, "That is definitely the same man who spoke to us at the museum." She nodded her head in agreement. They both felt a chill go down their spines and shivered together as if on cue. They walked slowly over to the team and shared the latest information. Jillian brought the flyer about Flannery Token over to the table for the team to view. One by one they studied the photo and read the obituary. They spoke about the possibilities. Bella said, "Given everything that has happened so far, I wonder if there could be a broken barrier somewhere in this town." "An opening that allows spirits to move freely back and forth." Matt said, "If that's true we really need to be careful." "We don't know what we might encounter." Jillian said sitting down after returning the article about Flannery Token back on the bulletin board, "That could explain the woman with the long flowing hair we saw at the Chateau." James stated thoughtfully, "Spirits often return to places that were meaningful to them when they were living." "Maybe the power of this town with the pain, suffering, despair, and the intensity of emotion that goes with these feelings acts almost like a magnet, attracting spirits back." Jillian responded, "Maybe certain spirits have unfinished business and return to achieve some sort of closure. This could be such a powerful desire that it could pull and draw them back to this location." Bella added, "I sense an intense darkness in this town. I have never experienced such an ominous feeling. I wonder what it might be like for spirits to be drawn back to a place without a real opportunity to resolve unfinished business. They are perhaps from another time, lost and without the opportunity to interact with loved ones. Leftover emotions from living like stress, anxiety, frustration, sadness, and just general angst. Emotions that are confusing and seemingly with no end increase over time due to lack of resolution. We all know what it is like to feel these emotions. It can be unbearable at times for the living. Who knows what happens to those who either choose not to move on-or in a state of confusion are left in limbo unable to move on." Chris added, "Don't forget those people who may have died violently or unexpectedly and do not understand what has happened to them. They would be stuck in a timeless limbo. I have always wondered if spirits who die unexpectedly and find themselves in this horrible situation are so confused, they do not understand the need to move on when the opportunity is presented." Aden spoke softly and said, "There is so much we do not understand about what happens when we die. I think it makes sense to believe that as we coexist with good and evil and what lies in-between in life, we could also coexist with good and evil and what lies in-between in death." The team sat for a few quiet moments and the server startled them when she asked if they needed anything else. They asked for more coffee as the discussion continued about the plan for the evening.

All agreed to focus on the Chateau for the first night of the investigation. They finished drinking coffee and when the server came back to give them the check, Jillian asked her where the residents of the town had gone. The server hesitated, brushed her long hair away from her face, and said, "This town has been dying out for a long time. Some of us were born and raised here and stayed but the people who could leave left. There are only about fifty of us living here now and we can barely make a living." "Some folks live within our city limits and commute to the next town over to work." She had a sad tone to her voice as she was speaking, and Jillian felt the sadness emanating.

The team left the diner and started the walk back to the Chateau. Mags happily walked close by occasionally sniffing by the side of the road.

It was late in the day as the team walked back up the long winding road leading to the Chateau. As they approached, a light blanket of darkness surrounded the large estate. It grew darker as they walked. Jillian looked at James and as he noticed her glance, he turned toward her and said, "I see the darkness and I feel it."

Once they arrived, the group walked together around the interior of the house to determine where to start the investigation. Video and sound recording equipment would be set up in the grand entry hall, the main staircase, and the upstairs hallway. They continued the walk around the large house to find other areas of interest. Mags was excited to run around and investigate and she led the way. The house had two main wings at the top of the stairs going right and left. Each wing had six bedrooms. The hallway connected at the backside of the house by another staircase. This staircase led up to an attic floor as well as downstairs connecting to the kitchen. This back staircase also led down past the kitchen to the basement.

Angie walked up the back stairs to the attic. She opened the attic door and said, "Of course, it would look like this." They all walked through the attic door. The team stood in the middle of an expansive room with old furniture and belongings covered with old dusty sheets. The contents of this room looked as if it had remained undisturbed for decades if not longer. Bella walked over, lifted a sheet, and started coughing as enormous amounts of dust lifted into the air. Underneath the sheet, she found old suitcases and framed pictures. They all shuddered and everyone with the exception of Aden needed to look away. The pictures were antique, old-style paintings of people. The pictures were dark and in poor condition and the people in the paintings had somber faces wearing old-style clothing. The condition of the pictures as well as the style of the paintings created an eerie almost evil appearance to the people depicted in them. There were three paintings. One of a middle-aged man, one of a middle-aged woman, and one painting with a family including the man and woman as well as three children. A young toddler boy and two older sisters who appeared to be twins.

Aden walked closer to the paintings and said, "Look at the eyes." "The eyes are almost black." Angie said, "The painting of the kids looks extra creepy." "It's the staring black eyes." Matt said, "They all look so unhappy. Typical of the paintings of the time. No one is ever smiling." The team stood, mesmerized by the old eerie-looking paintings. Jillian said, "This must be the Luster family whose ancestors founded the town." "The toddler could be William Luster." Nick said, "Well this sets the tone for a lovely investigation." They all laughed uncomfortably and continued to study the room. Bella said, "When we are in this room at night- we will need to be careful." "With only minimal light this room will cast many shadows." This statement contained many meanings and it hung in the air after she finished speaking adding to the ominous feeling the team members carried.

Angie walked around the attic room and lifted a pile of old suitcases off a stack. Underneath she found large, dusty trunks made of a combination of leather, wood, and metal. She called out, "Hey, look what I found!" The group stood over the trunks and, observing the apparent age Nick said, "I wonder what could be inside?" Jillian, having second thoughts answered, "We cannot open these. These are not our belongings. We have permission from the owner to look around and investigate but that does not include going through personal items." Matt said, "She did not specifically tell us we could not look through boxes and trunks though, right? She will not know if we place everything back where we found it." Jillian felt very apprehensive about this possible invasion of privacy. James asked, "Will our curiosity win over the ethical dilemma?" Jillian, James, Bella, Chris, Nick, Matt, Aden, and Angie stood around the trunks looking at one another. Nick said, "We must look. We might find important clues. No one will know!" He bent over one of the large trunks, unbuckled the leather straps, and pulled the iron hook out. He slowly opened the trunk lid. The low-level lighting in the attic forced them to use flashlights to see the contents in the trunk. Nick pulled out antique clothing including women's dresses that were faded and worn, a pair of kid's pants with holes in the knees, and a young girl's lacey bonnet with ties underneath. From the very bottom, he pulled out a large, long black hooded garment and held it up. It was dusty and smelled like mildew. He wondered, "What was this used for?" Placing the hooded cape or robe-like garment back he kept digging in the trunk. Nick pulled out a tattered and worn hooded garment with a decayed and frayed rope belt. He held it up and the group touched it. The fabric was heavy and coarse to touch. It had holes from age, but the original shape of the garment was identifiable. The hooded garment had long sleeves and wide cuffs. This hooded cape or robe had a different and unique smell to it. Chris took a whiff when holding it and exclaimed, "Wow, this smells as if it has been buried in the dirt for a long time. It smells like minerals, and it is musty. It reminds me of the smell of swamp mud or maybe peat." Matt asked, "What was the purpose of a brown hooded cape made of heavy wool? This looks much older compared to the other clothes in the trunk." Jillian said, "The black robe looks like a robe that might have been used in certain dark rituals. Maybe the brown hooded robe was also. We will never know for sure." Nick placed the brown robe back in the trunk and closed the lid.

Nick slid the next trunk over, unbuckled the straps, and pulled the iron hook out. He opened the lid and started lifting out smaller boxes. He opened one of the boxes and took out what appeared to be antique photos. The photos had a yellowed, tinny appearance. Nick studied an antique-looking photo of two children standing next to a younger child sitting in a chair. The standing children had short, dark hair, and wore old-fashioned clothes including long pants, long-sleeved shirts with high collars, and ankle-high boots. The child sitting in the chair between them was holding a stuffed bear and looked as if he was sleeping. Bella looking over Nick's shoulder sighed and said, "I know what this is. These are death photos. This was quite common when photography was new. It was a way to honor the dead and have a record of them as a family member before photography was more common. This child in the middle has passed away. The boys standing next to him are probably his brothers." They passed around the photo with curiosity. James handed the photo back to Nick and asked, "Isn't that kind of morbid?' Bella answered, "Life was difficult back then and death was much more common. This was an action that helped families mourn and honor the dead."

Jillian took out another photo and studied it. This was a photo of a woman reclining in bed dressed in a formal dress with her hands clasped on her lap. She handed it around and took out another framed photo. This was a photo of an entire family dressed in formal attire with a noticeably clear image of a man sitting in the middle. Two family members had their hands on his shoulders with one person holding one of the sitting man's hands. Angie asked, "Is the man sitting down deceased?" Bella answered, "Yes probably." The group looked at these photos quietly and the mood became gloomy and morose. There were so many of these death photos Jillian and Nick decided to stop taking them out. There were different families and the photos seemed to cover a span of time based on the clothing. Matt asked, "Why do you think there are so many of these photos in one place? Why would they be stored here?" Chris answered, "It's hard to say. The Chateau is so old, that this could be a combination of leftover belongings from families who left town, died off, and had no relatives to leave the photos with. Somehow, the photos ended up here." It was a mystery they probably would not solve, and Nick placed the photos back and closed the lid. As he did this a loud bang startled them. An item stacked in the back next to the wall fell. Aden said, "Wow, we are all a bit skittish right now!" Jillian felt her heart pounding and was creeped out by looking at the death photos. Matt, sensing everyone was on edge from looking at the photos said, "Let's shake it off and move on." The team walked out and closed the door behind them with a loud bang.

They walked down the back staircase and followed it lower to the basement. Chris opened the door and they all followed. Another long staircase led them to a large unfinished space. The basement had a dirt floor, and the light was so dim they could barely see. It was filled with old furniture and bulky items that could not be carried up the stairs to the attic. The basement smelled like dirt and dampness combined with mildew and stale smoke from an old stone fireplace located in the corner. Matt commented, "This must have been used as a workroom many years ago and the fireplace was used to heat the room." The fireplace had a stone mantle and as Matt walked closer, he could see old taxidermy birds covered in dust sitting on the mantle. They were large black birds with shiny feathers covered in dust. Nick walked over to a sheet covering an old piano. He lifted part of the sheet and touched a few keys. The sound echoed throughout the basement. The piano made a warped, twangy, and muted sound when he hit the keys. Angie said, "Of course, the piano would sound like that. Old creepy piano sounds." Aden answered, "Let's keep walking around."

Jillian walked over to the fireplace and noticed a loose stone on the lower step. She used her foot and jiggled the loose stone. She bent down and lifted the large stone out uncovering what appeared to be a small compartment or storage area. She continued to dig out the surrounding loose stones feeling compelled to discover what this space was. It felt eerily similar to the most recent Edin house investigation and her discovery of important old journals and books. She used the flashlight to peer inside the exposed space. She reached in and grabbed the edges of what felt like books. By now the group had formed around her watching inquisitively.

She pulled out three books. They were very worn, the covers faded, and the pages were yellowed and curled. The books felt almost wet to the touch and damp from being stored in the cool, dank basement with the dirt floor. The team stood still focused on the interesting find. Jillian looked at the book with the dusty black cover first. In faded gold letters the cover read Incantations in Darkness. She looked at the second book with the faded red cover that read Curses Book One. The third book with a faded yellow cover read Spells Book Two. They all looked at these books and the eerie silence became filled with curious chatter.

James found himself thinking about the success the Lusters had in this town at the expense of the residents and those who worked for the family company. This finding could be confirmation that the family's success was linked to the practice of dark magic. They would need to take time to study the books tomorrow.

Following the book discovery, the team decided to take a break and then reconvene at sunset to start the overnight investigation. They quietly stepped back up the staircase and walked down the long hallway to the bedrooms.

Chapter 7

The Understated

Jillian had suggested they all retire back to their rooms for a little while before starting the investigation. She believed the house was most active later at night and they were more likely to catch evidence if they waited. She was also feeling tired.

Jillian and James were sitting on the bed with Mags stretched out near their feet. They decided to set phone alarms for 1 hour to take a quick nap. James fell asleep immediately and Jillian stared at the ceiling thinking about everything they had been through over the past couple of days. She winced as she shifted positions and the pain reminded her of the details regarding her injury. She tried to push away the specific thoughts and memory about the creature and the graphic recall of how the injury happened. She could easily bring herself right back to those moments. The fear and horror she felt and the searing pain. The memory and the feeling of something evil clawing inside her and the warm blood dripping down her back. It was hard to ignore and impossible to forget. In addition, Jillian could not get the accident experience out of her head. She continued to relive those moments and felt deeply troubled by the car accident victims and the last words they spoke. It was not surprising that with all these thoughts rattling around in her head while she was trying to relax and rest, she was not settling down enough. After trying relaxation exercises for a few minutes Jillian succeeded in temporarily calming her mind. Thoroughly exhausted and even with so many distractions she eventually drifted to sleep.

She found herself standing next to the wrecked car on the snowy cliff. Leaning on the open driver's side door Jillian was looking in at the severely injured driver slumped over the wheel. Snow was falling around her, and she felt the chill in the air. The feeling of dread, sorrow, fear and impending doom overcame her as she stood shivering. The sense of helplessness was heavy knowing she could do nothing to save the driver of the car. She jumped when he moved. His head slowly turned to look at her. She could see a black aura that turned to red and back to black in just a few seconds. Then she started to smell the gas and see smoke as the car ignited into flames. This all felt remarkably familiar. Or did it? As the flames grew around and inside the car, she was frozen staring at the injured driver. She should have felt the urge to run from the car and away from the flames. Instead, she was immobile and unable to move her feet no matter how hard she tried. Understanding the car was going to explode in a matter of seconds, the panic took over. She was transfixed, staring at the driver. As she looked, she felt the adrenaline increasing and creating energy. Her body needed to move and the need to move away and escape was intense, while simultaneously a strong unknown force was compelling her to stay. Jillian broke out in a sweat from the heat of the growing fire, and the physical and emotional stress of the situation. A darkness seeped in all around her, and she thought she saw movement next to the driver. Looking closer, she could see red eyes staring at her from the passenger side of the car. The smoke was becoming thick inside and around the car, but the eyes continued to stare at her. She could not move as her eyes were locked on the being's stare. She could not make out what it looked like. Just a grey mass with red eyes. The eyes were liquid and they appeared to be in motion. Red liquid swishing around in dark eye sockets. The being was surrounded by a brilliant red aura that was growing around it. Then she heard a guttural, low growl growing louder. The growl turned into a shrill screech and then a low growl again. She covered her ears as it became louder. She felt the urge to run but still could not move. The smoke was becoming thick, and her eyes were burning. Then it spoke to her. It said, "You will never stop this. You and the others will die searching for answers." It spoke using sounds she would not describe as vocal sounds. It was almost speaking through a growl. The sound reverberated in her head and through her hands still covering her ears. It growled and then screeched louder as if becoming impatient with her. She knew this was an important moment and somehow knew it was an opportunity. The danger and the evil were unmistakable. This being wanted to communicate with her. It was a dire warning.

Jillian tried to quickly sort through her thoughts, and overcoming her fear she took a breath and said, "What do you want?" The creature hesitated and then laughed a horrible, loud, guttural, and then screechy laugh. She screamed from the pain of the noise the creature made. Her ears felt as if they were bleeding. When she stopped screaming, she heard a familiar sound in the distance. The car, smoke, and the creature with the liquid red eyes and the red aura faded away. The angry screeching and growling faded and became distant. She heard her phone alarm and opened her eyes to see James sitting beside her shaking her awake. He looked concerned and almost scared.

She sat up and shook her head. Mags jumped up and licked her face. It took her a few minutes to realize she had been dreaming again. She looked at James and he gasped. She panicked and asked, "What is wrong?" He told her to look in the mirror. She jumped out of bed, ran to the bathroom, and turned on the light. She gazed at her image and took a step back. Her eyes were blood red. She took a step toward the mirror to get a closer look. Her eyes had turned to a red liquid, and she could see the red swishing around inside her eye sockets. She screamed hysterically and then felt James shaking her awake. She opened her eyes, and she was still on the bed. Mags ran up to her and licked her face. She jumped up and ran to the bathroom, turned on the light, and looked at her reflection. Her eyes appeared normal. She was sweating and breathing hard.

James was standing behind her when she turned around. "You clearly had another dream," he stated. She turned to face him and fell into his arms. The tears fell from her eyes as she felt relief knowing it was just another dream. She felt safe with James and understood she was ok for the moment. It felt like the immense cloud of horror, anxiety, and dread just blew away in that instant. James waited for Jillian to collect herself to hear about the dream. She said, "James, the dreams are becoming more powerful and intense. There is something about this place and the energy it is emanating."

Jillian told James about the creature she saw in the car. She felt it was a dark spirit trying to communicate a message and an ominous warning intended for her and the team. It might be the same spirit that spoke to her in the prison through the inmate and spoke through the car accident victim. The spirit that said, "Why are you wasting your time with this person when you should be speaking with me?" James was not sure how to respond. Jillian was very shaken by this experience. He felt helpless over how to help her with dangerous dreams that can harm her. It was emotional and physical danger. They both sat quietly on the bed with Mags between them thinking the same thing. Who or what was the creature Jillian saw in her dream trying to communicate with her?

While James and Jillian were discussing her dream, Aden was sleeping soundly in his room. He was deep in a dream that brought him back to the family house he lived in when he was young. He was about seven years old and sleeping in his childhood room. Everything was in place just as he remembered it. The white desk and chair and the bookcase with his favorite books. Two shelves of the bookcase were crowded with his plastic block sculpture masterpieces. The bean bag chair on the floor, with art supplies scattered about. The poster of planets and the blue paint on the walls. He was stretched out on the bed as his seven-year-old self -awakened out of a sound sleep. He thought he heard a noise from somewhere in his childhood room and opened his eyes. He carefully scanned the room as he began to feel panic. Suddenly Aden was flooded with the emotions of a frightened seven-year-old and the familiar feelings came rushing back. The nightmare of his childhood dealing with the fear of what might happen to him at night. A seven-year-old dealing with evil and the unknown by himself.

He stayed very still, listening for any sound. His breathing was erratic and shaky as he trembled under the blankets. The room became very cold, and he could see his breath hanging in the air like smoke. These signs were not new. As a seven-year-old boy, Aden had been dealing with hauntings and unusual, unexplainable events since he was a toddler. His fear was justifiable. Just a few moments in that room in his dream brought back the vivid memories of years of childhood torment all at once. He had tears in his eyes as he cried out from his bed. He felt the bed shake from something moving underneath. He could hear deep, raspy breathing coming from under his bed. The dread, the absolute terror overwhelmed him. He was frozen for a few moments hiding under a blanket. He took a deep breath and uncovered his head. Aden could still hear raspy, slow breathing under his bed. He slowly sat up and leaned over to get a quick look. On his stomach, stretched out across the side of the bed he leaned over closer to the floor to get a better look. He could not see well due to the low light in his room created by the moon shining through the window. Sitting up, he stepped down off the bed and crouched on the floor. He was shaking and crying, and at the same time compelled to see what was under the bed. He hoped he would find nothing but had a deep and familiar gut feeling about what he might find. He crouched down and peered under the bed. A long, gray, bony hand with long thin fingers reached out and grabbed his arm. Screaming, and thrashing, Aden was dragged under the bed.

He opened his eyes and was standing in the dark, outside his childhood home. He was shaking from the cold, the adrenaline, and the fear. He was confused and had no memory of how he ended up outside by himself at night in the cold. Wiping the tears off his face with his pajama sleeve, he walked up the front steps to the front door. The door was locked so he proceeded to ring the doorbell and knock. Aden desperately wanted to see his parents at the door. Horrified and experiencing the increasing feelings of desperation and panic, Aden rapidly knocked on the door until the door suddenly opened. With a sigh of relief, he rushed through the door expecting to see his parents. Instead, he was greeted by a creature with glowing red eyes. Aden screamed and sat up, sweating, and shaking. He looked around to notice he was in his room at the Chateau. It was a dream. He was having a dream.

There was a knock on the door. Aden collected himself, walked over, and opened the door to find Angie. She said they were meeting at the entrance of the hotel. She noticed he was pale with deep circles around his eyes. He told her he had a terrible dream, but it was fine now. He followed her down the hall and to the main staircase to meet the group.

Chapter 8

Dark Surprises

The group stood under the dim light in the entryway of the Chateau. There was excitement in the air along with trepidation as they discussed the plan for the investigation. Jillian felt drawn to the attic and volunteered to start there. James agreed to join her. Angie would monitor the cameras at the central control station set up in the back room behind the front desk. Chris and Bella chose to start in the basement while Aden, Nick and Matt would investigate the upstairs hallway and bedrooms. They would all bring walkies and stay in communication.

They joined together in a circle and offered best wishes to one another. Chris spoke up and said, "We all know the risks and need to be on guard and careful. We understand the possibilities and need to keep our mission and goals in mind. We are gaining information to help understand and fight against the darkness. Let us protect one another in the process." They looked at one another in silence, paused, and then broke the circle and walked to the planned locations.

Angie sat down in front of the camera monitors. She checked the entrance, the basement, the attic, and the upstairs hallway and bedrooms. Everything looked quiet as she watched the group getting settled in the various locations.

Chris and Bella started slowly down the dark, creaking stairs to the basement. As they stepped carefully, a loud sound with a warped and muted twang stopped them in their tracks. Bella gasped and shivered. Chris placed his hand on her shoulder, and she released a breath. They heard the echo of the piano key and then silence. They stood still on the stairs as if on pause, waiting for something else to happen. The basement was quiet, and they continued down the stairs. The smell hit Bella immediately. The stale air, the dampness, and the mineral smell from the dirt floor. The smell of stagnant smoke from a fireplace that had not been used in a century.

Angie called them on the walkie. She reported getting the piano key sound on the video. She could not determine why or how the piano made that sound. Bella and Chris walked slowly over to the piano and looked around. Bella found an old candle had fallen onto the keys of the piano. They both sighed in relief. She walked toward the camera and showed Angie the candle. Bella wondered how the candle had fallen. Chris said. "I think maybe when we walked down the stairs the old soft wood creaked and moved creating a vibration in the room." "Maybe the piano moved and shook a bit and the candle fell." Angie listened to the explanation and wondered about the plausibility.

Bella and Chris were not convinced about this explanation however for now it helped them feel less anxious about being in the basement. They walked around and Bella found an aged wooden rocking chair to sit on. She decided to sit quietly and get a feel for the room. Chris sat on the piano bench and they both fell silent.

Angie continued to watch the monitors for any unusual activity. Aden, Nick, and Matt walked slowly up the long front staircase and hesitated at the top of the stairs. They looked down the long hallway leading to the bedrooms. Nick turned around to look over the staircase and toward the front door. The large windows in the lower grand hallway gave a beautiful panoramic view of the town of Susurrous Pines at night. The lights glowing from below looked bright and beautiful with the dark mountains all around. He said, "This town is really quite charming. It's sad so many residents have left." Nick turned back and they started down the hall.

There were many bedrooms off the upper hallway wing and they each chose a bedroom to investigate. Aden chose the bedroom with William Luster's name above the door. Nick chose the room that appeared to have once been a nursery with a shelf of old antique dolls and a bench seat at the window. Matt chose the grand master bedroom with a large poster bed and fireplace. They all sat down in the rooms to get their bearings.

Jillian and James walked up the long back staircase to the attic. The stairs creaked and as they approached the top of the staircase the strong musty smell was identifiable even before they entered. Walking up the stairs James noticed it gradually became darker as they ascended. When they reached the top, the light was so absent they needed to use flashlights to find the doorknob to enter the room.

James turned the doorknob, pushed the creaking door open, and they slowly entered. The lights in the attic were far too dim and they used an extra flashlight set up in the middle on a table. Jillian used her flashlight to pan around the room squinting her eyes to see more clearly. She could see the dust particles reflecting in the light as their footsteps disturbed the thick layer of dust on the floor. The floor felt slick with the heavy layer of dust and dirt. Jillian sat on a wooden bench and James sat on the floor. They both remained quiet to get a feel for the room.

Angie continued to monitor the screens, with Mags at her feet, anticipating something might happen. Angie felt extremely uncomfortable and anxious and fully expected they might have a busy and unpredictable night. The house was quiet, and Angie could hear Mags breathing, her tail softly thumping the floor as she dreamed. She watched Nick on the video as he stood up and walked over to the shelf with the dolls. He picked up his walkie and said, "I swear I just saw one of the dolls move its head. I feel totally creeped out." Angie rewound the tape to see if she could see any of the dolls move. Nick stood, watching the dolls. Angie used slow-motion and jumped when she saw a doll's head move. It was dark in the room, but she could see the doll's head move to one side. Chills went down her spine and she shivered. She watched the tape one more time and gasped. The walkie was still on, and Nick asked what was happening in a slightly panicked voice. Angie looked in horror as the doll's eyes opened and the eyes moved to look directly at the camera.

She said, "Nick, not only did the doll's head move to one side but the eyes moved and looked directly at the camera!" Nick turned and walked out of the bedroom feeling shaky. Matt and Aden had been listening and met him in the hallway. Matt said, “That is awesome!” Aden said, “We need to go back to that room while it’s still active and see what else might happen.” All three went back into the room and studied the shelf of dolls while Nick pointed out the doll that moved. It was a small doll with curled shoulder-length brown hair, a faded pink lace dress, and pink matching faded hair bows. It had pink frilly socks and brown shoes. The doll had what appeared to be a porcelain face with small features and brown eyes that opened and closed when it was moved up and down. Matt picked the doll up, looked around the shelf, and then placed it back. He said, “Why are old dolls so creepy?” Jillian, James, Bella, and Chris all listened to what was happening and stayed in place.

In the attic, Jillian was feeling very uneasy. She was drawn there for a reason and was experiencing intense anxiety and a sense of dread. She found herself staring at the dust particles floating around in the light. James shifted and she jumped at the sound. He asked her if she was all right. She nodded and stayed silent. She stared at the light in the center of the room and found her eyes wandering to a dark corner behind a sheet covering old furniture. She stood up and walked over to the corner to run her hands over the walls. The walls were constructed of old plaster, and they were covered with layers of dust and dirt. James asked, “Did you find something over there?” She stepped back and used her flashlight to study the wall. “I’m not sure.” She walked back over to the chair. Nothing stood out about that corner as she sat back in the chair while continuing to find herself compelled to look over in that direction.

Suddenly Jillian had a vivid memory of when she was younger, at the original haunted house- the Edin house when she was sixteen. The haunting experience that was the catalyst for this journey she pursued to find answers. Jillian closed her eyes as her heartbeat sped up. This attic was remarkably like the attic in the Edin house. With her eyes closed, she could picture that old room and the horrifying shuffling noises. She felt as if she was there again. She could smell the room and see the shadows. The extreme fear was taking over, and she felt frozen in place. But her old memory ended there, and a new experience began. She was hiding behind an antique dresser, and she slowly peeked around and found herself looking in the dark corner. She stood up to see what appeared to be a shadow in the corner. Shaking she walked over hoping it was her imagination but needing to find out for sure. She stood in the dark corner and saw nothing out of the ordinary. Suddenly she could see long bony, thin, grey arms emerge out of the wall. A head and body followed the arms flowing out of the wall like liquid. This creature had a brilliant red aura surrounding it. The aura was growing. There was red liquid dripping all around the creature, and red liquid dripping down the wall. She screamed and started to turn and run away but the bony, thin, gray arms grabbed her. The creature had partially emerged from the wall. As it pulled her toward the wall, she turned back to find herself looking directly into the red eyes of this creature. It had sunken eyes and grey wrinkled skin and she desperately tried to break free of its grasp. She told herself this could not be real however she could not break free. It felt all too real. She could hear James from far away yelling "Jillian, what is happening?" "Wake up, wake up!" She could not break free of the creature's grip and the sharp bony hands were cutting into her arms as it pulled her towards the wall. She shrieked in pain, screaming over and over while scrambling to break free. The creature pulled her through the wall, and she felt herself falling, falling into the dark oblivion.

Chapter Nine

Deep Secrets

Jillian slowly opened her eyes to find she was surrounded by the group. Angie, Matt, Nick, Aden, Bella Chris, and James all stood around her looking genuinely concerned. James said. "Thank God she is waking up. I was about to call emergency services!"

Jillian was flat out on the floor on her back and slowly sat up trying to clear her head. She was still in the attic of the Chateau, but a few minutes ago she was back at the Edin house with the creature that pulled her through the wall. She asked James, "What happened?" James said, "You were sitting on the chair, and then you started screaming and fell to the ground and we couldn't bring you back to us!" She had complete recall of her memory at this point and stood up with purpose. Everyone backed up to give her space and she walked over to that dark corner again. She moved her hands along the wall until she felt grooves. She wiped the dust and dirt away and followed the grooves with her hands. As she did, it became clear there was a hidden door she was uncovering. They all joined in and brushed away the dust. Matt said, "It looks like this was some sort of a door at one time and it was covered up with plaster. They all looked at one another and Jillian said, "We need to open this up. I just had an intense vision, and it was like a waking dream. It was a clue."

James looked around for a tool they could use to break away the plaster. He found an old fireplace poker and placed the edge into one part of the groove to pry it apart from the wall. The plaster was old, and it crumbled easily. They all grabbed items they could find in the attic to help James break away the remaining plaster. When they finished a door was showing with a hole for a doorknob. They stood back and looked at the old wooden door. The wall with the door was at the edge of the room and at the exterior wall of the house. Chris said, "Where could this door lead to?" "We are at the far end of the house. Why would a door lead to the outside on the top floor?"

Jillian spoke up and said, "In my memory, a creature pulled me through this wall, and I fell very, very far down below." "Let's open the door and see where it leads." She put her hand inside the hole where the doorknob used to be and pulled hard. The door swung open making a loud creaking noise. Dust and stale air entered the room and they all coughed. She pointed her flashlight through the doorway and the group gasped. There was a steep, narrow stone staircase leading straight down. There was a long two-sided wooden railing that lined both sides of the staircase all the way down. She looked at everyone and said, "We need to find out where this goes!" "We need a volunteer to stay upstairs and guard the door so we don't get locked in since we don't know where this will lead us." Angie volunteered to stay along with Aden who felt much trepidation about going down that staircase. Matt, Chris, Bella, Nick, James, and Jillian would all go down the stairs. They felt safe with more people going but agreed if the structure seemed unsound, they would not continue.

James volunteered to go first, and Jillian said, "Let me go, I got us into this situation." He understood she needed to do this and said he would follow closely behind her. The stairs were very dark and descending the staircase would be like stepping into a cave. Chris rigged a bright flashlight at the top of the stairs pointing down. They all brought flashlights and lined up to start down the stairs. Jillian leaned over to look down the steep stairs one more time before descending. Even with the flashlights, this would be a challenge. She pushed back the thoughts about her vision, or dream as she was not sure what to call it. A creature pulled her through the wall. Is this creature still waiting for them somewhere in the depths of this house? She needed to find out why this message was sent to her. Someone or something is trying to communicate with her, but why? James interrupted her thoughts and asked if she was ok to proceed. She turned around and realized everyone was watching her calmly but expectantly. Jillian took a breath and stepped onto the first step holding the railing with both hands while also keeping a tight grip on her flashlight. Her feet slipped on the dusty stone stairs. She said, "Everyone be careful, the stairs are very dusty and slick." She stood for a moment looking around. She noticed markings on the wall and pointed her flashlight. The walls were blanketed in dust, but she could make out rudimentary drawings on the old wooden walls. "What is this?" There were hooded figures drawn in black, walking in a line following the wall all the way as far as she could see down the stairs. She shivered with a chill looking at these drawings, as she was about to step down the stairs. Jillian said, "Check out the drawings on the wall going down the stairs." She started descending, slowly, one step at a time. After a few steps, she looked up to see James step on the first stairs. The stairway was extremely small and cramped and James barely fit in the space.

Jillian continued slowly down the stairs. By now the rest of the group was on the staircase working their way down. Jillian guessed she had passed three floors at this point and thought she should be nearing the basement level. She assumed the staircase would end at the basement however it appeared to keep going. She looked up to see the rest of the group following her and she kept going. James said, "Jillian where does this end?" She noticed he sounded concerned and she was beginning to think this was a bad idea, however she pushed these thoughts away and kept going. She passed the basement level and continued moving down. About twenty stairs past the basement, she finally stepped on solid ground.

With both feet on solid ground on the stone floor, she turned around to see she was standing in a small room. She stepped away from the stairs to give the group room to step down into the space. They all stood together in this small room looking around. "This is incredible!" Matt said. James pointed his flashlight at the wall next to the stairs. He could see the drawing of the hooded figures, and where the drawing stopped at the bottom of the stairs. "What do these drawings mean?" He asked. Chris answered, "They certainly add to the creepiness of this space." Bella said, "I wonder what they used this for?" Jillian looked at James and he knew what she was thinking. He would touch the wall and see if he could see any images.

Before James had an opportunity to touch the wall Bella spoke up, "I am feeling intense darkness here. Something very terrible happened in this area." "I sense we are not alone, and there may be many spirits around us." Chris looked at her with concern. He understood her connection with the paranormal and her ability to make a connection with spirits beyond their realm. It was a gift and a curse. Every time she used this gift it chipped away at her humanity. It created a vulnerability and with each experience caused more damage to her defenses and her armor. At the same time, each experience with the other dimension increased the spirit's attraction to her. A snowball effect that created the pull for more interaction and more exposure. Chris feared for Bella over time. He wondered what will happen to her as her defenses are broken down.

As Chris was deep in his own thoughts, James was using his flashlight to look more closely at the wall starting where the drawings of the hooded figures ended. The group watched the light as he moved it along the wall. He stopped at a point near the stairs where he noticed another drawing of a hooded figure. He followed the wall next to the first drawing to see a continuation of the hooded figures. The drawings seemed to depict a metamorphosis. Each drawing of the hooded figure was different. The figure was transitioning into something else. The group watched the flashlight as it moved along the succession of drawings. Jillian took a deep breath as she followed the light to the final drawing. The hooded figure was becoming increasingly more monstrous. It became elongated, growing thinner and thinner. It became hunched over with long thin bony arms and legs that now protruded from the hooded robe. The head changed shape and was long and thin with sunken eyes. The skin hung loosely from the arms, legs, and the face. It had long wispy grey hair. The final drawing showed the figure hunched over and looking at the viewer. It was the eyes. The red eyes. Jillian felt herself breathing fast with her heart pounding in her throat.

Jillian said, "This is the monster that pulled me down through the wall. I suspect one like it also injured me during my dream." James spoke up and said, "We have seen similar monsters/spirits before. At the Edin house investigation." Chris spoke up and said, "So maybe this is where it all began." Matt said, "We need more information. We must find out what happened here."

James decided to touch the drawing on the wall. He moved to place his hand on the final monstrous figure that was drawn. Jillian caught his hand and said, "James please be careful. This could be a new level of darkness for us." He turned to look at her and he gave her an affectionate hug. He said, "Jillian don't worry. I am always careful." She knew that he could not protect himself and the others from the powerful darkness they were beginning to understand. She could only hope they would be prepared to deal with whatever they encountered. She also felt deep down a sense of impending doom that they were about to uncover an evil, unlike anything they had ever seen before.

Chris watched Jillian and James as they comforted each other and hoped their bond would make them stronger. He was also aware that the closer they came to finding answers the more everyone in the group would be tested. Vulnerabilities might be exposed, and if the darkness is allowed in there is no predicting what might happen.

James turned to face the wall and touched the final drawing. It was quiet at first. The group braced themselves knowing that sometimes the environment could become stormy when James allowed these experiences. The air started to move around the room. A wind developed and blew around them getting stronger and stronger. They stood arm and arm holding one another upright. The wind became louder and louder and then suddenly stopped. James fell to his knees and the air was still. Jillian knelt touching his shoulder. "Are you ok?" She asked.

James sat up leaning against the wall trying to understand

the rush of images he just received. The group understood he needed space to collect his thoughts. His head was pounding, and he intentionally tried to slow down and control his breathing. He opened his eyes and said, "That was very intense." "I saw a lot of images and I am not sure I understand what I saw. I will try to explain it."

They all stood very still waiting for James to start. He said, "I saw a little boy dressed in old-looking clothes from another time. He appeared to have a privileged life living in a large house and playing in the expansive backyard. I saw images of him growing up. Eating at a long, large table with his parents and siblings. He was special and born with powerful gifts. He was an integral. Born with gifts to save humanity from the darkness. As the images came to me, they started turning darker. He played by himself more often. He appeared to be practicing dark magic using candles and sacrificing small animals. He did this secretly and found it made him increasingly more powerful. He had books he used that he found in secret hiding places within his house. The Chateau was his house." Jillian said, "You are speaking of William Luster. We found some of those books today!" James looked at her and nodded. He continued. "As William grew up, he became increasingly obsessed with dark magic and eventually became overwhelmed by it. He succumbed to the temptations and was drawn to the power. Darkness followed him. By the time he reached adulthood, it had transformed him into something else. He was able to portray himself as a successful businessperson taking over for his father. While all the time secretly practicing dark magic with evil overtaking him." "There is something else. The town was overtaken by greed, violence, pain, and loss. This gave William even more power. It fed the darkness and as the town transformed so did William." Jillian said, "He became the embodiment of evil." James said, "When the town died and nothing was left, the Luster family had to leave." Jillian said, "The Edin house. They moved to the Edin house." This was the connection to the Edin house investigation. Matt said, "There was so much darkness in Susurrous Pines, and this is where it all began. It makes sense that William Luster could still be connected and attached to this area. Even more so than the Edin House area."

Bella said, "I know what happened here. I believe this tunnel somehow leads from this room to the mines built into the mountains." She shined her flashlight toward the far wall and the group could see the opening to a tunnel. She added, "Something is guiding us, directing us to walk through these tunnels. But there were tragedies that occurred here in the mines. There is a lot of death and pain." "Feelings of betrayal, and intense anger and hatred." Chris looked at Bella intensely as she spoke. She had the ability to obtain information due to the unique connection she experienced with the other side, or the other dimension. They did not understand how she possessed this ability, and she was still in the process of learning how to use it. Her perceptions were usually correct, and he took her seriously when she spoke.

Suddenly, there was a loud bang coming from the tunnel. The sound of moaning, and a dragging noise. Jillian instinctively understood they needed to leave immediately. The group was not prepared to deal with what was approaching them. They all understood the danger. Fear took over and they scrambled to the staircase. Bella went first, then Matt, Jillian, Chris, Nick, and James. The moaning noise was getting louder and changed to a shrieking and then a low raspy growl. The dragging sound moving closer. The group moved as quickly as possible up the dark stairs. It was a long climb and James could hear it following them. He could hear something on the stairs behind him. "Everyone move faster! It's on the stairs!" They were breathing hard and panicking. James was moving as quickly as possible while looking back waiting for whatever was following them to catch up. Bella reached the top and Angie and Aden helped her out of the stairway. They all helped each person out of the narrow space until James finally appeared. They grabbed him and he fell into the room. The door was slammed shut and they moved an old table to block it- hopefully preventing something on the other side from getting in. They were breathing hard and listening for any sign of what was following them. It was quiet. Jillian breathed a sigh of relief, and they all took a breath. Angie and Aden looked at them and Angie asked, "What happened?" Bella said, "Let's go downstairs and we will fill you in." "I need to get out of this attic."

The night was almost over with dawn just minutes away. They all organized in the front hall. Exhausted and shaky, the group decided sleep was necessary with a plan to meet up later in the morning. There were hours of video footage left to review before planning the next investigation. They were fascinated with the tunnels discovered and all agreed the tunnels needed to be explored more extensively the following night. Without much more discussion the group departed to the rooms to sleep.

Chapter 10

The Familiar

Bella could see it in the distance ahead. Images emerged as she walked closer but remained unfocused as she strained her eyes. She moved her head slowly up and down, left, and right with her hands cupped over her eyes studying the horizon. Her pace picked up. The view was just out of reach as the excitement and frustration increased. She needed to see what was on that horizon- everything depended on it. She glanced nervously behind her and could see the others separating. They were slowly moving away from one another and from her. The distant figures were less visible as they were fading as she strained to see them through the mist and fog. The figures appeared as small distorted gray shadows barely identifiable while slowly disappearing. All that was eventually visible behind her was the growing darkness.

She was alone. Bella could see the shadowy darkness enter her vision from the periphery. She felt the uncontrollable urge to run. The panic, fear, and isolation took hold as she ran, and the darkness spread closer. The sound of her feet hitting the dirt road was pounding in her head. The burst of energy gave her hope for progress.

She took a deep breath, looking again toward the horizon, and noticed a bright light solely emerging like a wave. The darkness was located behind her and the bright light ahead. She stopped short, out of breath with beads of sweat on her forehead and cheeks. A moment almost frozen in time if not for the heavy breathing and dripping sweat. She swept her hair away from her face and studied the sweeping light approaching her. It was now or never. The darkness felt familiar and almost comforting. The light was welcoming, and it too felt comforting. Bella knew in her heart what was right. She knew deep down in her soul the consequences of the path she was to choose. The temptation and the pull were present. Why would she ever consider such an alternative? Was it really a choice? Were forces at work that might impact her ability to take control of her fate? She asked herself these questions while standing on the path.

Bella could finally see her destiny and believed in some way it was finally accepting her. The direction of her future was determined by her, or so she believed. Now she must walk into it and bathe in the light of decision.

Bella opened her eyes with the light shining on her face from the window. She was still in bed, with Chris next to her. Her head was foggy from a deep sleep. She understood the importance of the images and dream and felt the pull toward the darkness. She needed to remain strong. There was something remarkably familiar about the need and the desire to allow the darkness in. Bella knew it was wrong, but the temptation was intense and relentless. She could not allow the evil to turn her. It had happened before to others. It happened to William Luster. She was beginning to understand.

Jillian showered while James slept. She stood letting the warm water flow over her with her eyes closed. She tried to free her mind for just a few minutes. Jillian felt the burden of her position and the responsibility carried by her, James, Bella, Chris, and the entire group. Discovering evil and attempting to stop it from entering and infiltrating our world. Preventing the scourge to preserve human existence. No matter how hard she tried to distract herself she could never be free from the heaviness of the responsibility.

Jillian stepped out of the shower, dried off, and dressed. She sat on the bed and Mags came over to greet her. Jillian leaned over to pat her head and rub her ears. Mags wagged her tail with approval leaning in for more. Her cell phone started ringing. She walked over to the nightstand, looked at the screen, and did not recognize the number. She answered the phone and the detective investigating the car accident identified himself. He said they identified the two men who died in the car accident and fire. The men were brothers and had been camping in the mountains while researching and investigating the old mines. They were bloggers and produced a show focused on uncovering old secrets and mysteries while investigating old historic sites. The brothers were working on a project about the old mines in the mountains surrounding Susurrous Pines. Their names were Colton and Steve Barrington. The Barrington brothers.

Jillian took the opportunity to question the detective about the unusual activity they had experienced in town, at the Chateau, and in the areas surrounding Susurrous Pines. The detective paused after she asked about what he knew of strange occurrences and experiences reported in and around Susurrous Pines. She waited for him to respond. He answered, "This town has a lot of history and much of it is not good. Terrible things have happened here over many years. Many residents and business owners have departed over time it feels like a ghost town. It is a dying town in many ways. These circumstances can lead to rumors and mystery. The few remaining residents are superstitious and feel an unusual attachment to this place. Due to the history, rumors, and mystery of Susurrous Pines, it attracts people like you and your group and like the Barrington brothers. If you are asking if I believe in ghosts, I will say no. Do I think strange occurrences have and do happen in this town? I will say yes." Detective Turner was not willing to elaborate on his answer, and Jillian could sense a defensiveness in his response. She understood the interview was finished and he would not be answering any more questions along this vein. She ended the call graciously thanking him for his time.

By now James was awake and she explained what the detective shared with her. They immediately opened laptops and began searching online for postings, and any videos they could find from the Barrington Brothers. The research came easily. The Barrington Brothers had a large following and they had been offering teasers about upcoming episodes. They spoke about Susurrous Pines and what they called "the haunted mines."

James and Jillian watched the clip of the teaser with intense focus. The clip mentioned an explosion event that occurred in the mines many years ago. It was a disaster that caused the death of miners including children. There was one woman missing from town who was also thought to have perished. The Barrington Brothers believed the spirits of the people killed were still haunting the mines. They had found articles and stories about hikers in the area reportedly seeing ghosts, shadow people, and hearing unexplained voices in the forest areas surrounding the mines. The clip was created with the use of dramatic footage in a forest, and scary suspenseful music.

She sat thinking about the Barrington brothers and what they must have seen and discovered in their investigation. She gasped slightly as she remembered her dream with the creature moving around in the car before it caught fire. She thought about those deep red eyes. She winced when remembering what the creature in the car said to her. The sound of its voice was still ingrained in her mind. Did this creature follow them out of the mines somehow? Did it attach itself to one of them? As she sat deep in thought Mags groaned in her sleep and shifted on the bed. Jillian jumped, as she was startled by the sound. Mags woke up when Jillian shook the bed and walked over to her. She put her head on Jillian's leg and looked up at her. Jillian held her sweet dog's head and gave her a kiss on the nose. Mags wagged her tail and sat up.

Jillian stood up and walked over to the window while James continued to search on his laptop. He looked up and watched her move to the window. He stood up with his messy, tousled long hair, and walked over to stand next to her. He placed his arms around her. She turned to face him and placed her arms around his neck. They passionately kissed and hugged close. She loved James with all of her being. It was not just his handsome face. She loved his soulful eyes, thoughtful and caring nature, his humor, and the unbreakable bond they shared. It was a once-in-a-lifetime connection and she never took it for granted. Jillian appreciated loving him every day even when they became distracted with these investigations and the risk endured on a regular basis.

Together they looked out onto the snow-covered mountains. It was a cloudy day and somewhat gray. Even with the dismal weather, it was beautiful. She said, "What a pretty landscape." As her eyes moved up the mountain closest to the hotel she could see the details of the trees, and the rocks and cliffs near the top. A coating of snow covered the mountain and the trees. Then she froze, staring at one tree line area near the top of the mountain. She focused her eyes and thought she saw movement in the trees. Dark figures moving high up in the trees. She could see large chunks of snow falling from the trees as the tree limbs were moving underneath the weight. James could feel the change in her posture and thought he felt Jillian trembling. Before he could inquire about what was happening, she quickly asked, "Look! In the trees. Do you see it?" He took a step closer to the window and scanned the forest areas. She asked him if he could see the movement in the trees. She pointed to where she was looking, and he stood still for a moment focusing. They both watched as the snow fell to the ground from the group of trees. The tree limbs were moving erratically and causing the snow on the limbs to clear off and fall to the ground in large mounds. They could not see enough detail at such a distance. Jillian felt immediately compelled to go to that specific location and investigate. She was not sure, but she thought the movement looked familiar. She had vivid memories of what she saw in the trees during the Edin house investigation. She shook her head instinctively to rid herself of those memories as she shivered from a chill. James paused and said, "You do not know. We are far away and the movement in the trees could be caused by large birds, squirrels, or other animals." She looked at him and said, "We must go there. I need to check that area out." James knew better than to argue with her when she was determined and compelled in this way. He also understood from experience that her gut reactions and instincts were often correct although he was sincere in his belief that this time the source of the movement in the trees could be something other than the supernatural or paranormal.

James contacted the group which involved waking them from a deep sleep and suggested they meet in the lobby to discuss the new plan for the day. He went down early to look for maps of the mountain areas around the hotel. He found old maps behind the front desk and unfolded them. He took out his phone and checked his maps and compared. The paper maps showed roads and details the phone maps did not display. He found a road that appeared to lead up to the mountain near the area where they saw the movement in the trees. By now the group was assembled in the great front hall. When James walked toward the group, he could hear Jillian telling them what she thought she saw in the trees. They were all on board to investigate that area if they could get there safely. James said, "I found a map with a road that looks like it will get us close to where we want to go. But we will need to bring the biggest SUV/truck we have. The road may not be in good condition. We will need to prepare for the possibility of a long hike depending on how close we can get." Chris said, "I wonder if we can find a better, more equipped truck in town?" He started making calls starting with the car repair shop. He was quickly able to secure a rental for the day that had enough passenger seating and was a better option for the mountain roads. They planned to meet in an hour after everyone gathered equipment and supplies.

A quick hour later the group met in front of the hotel with Mags happily following behind. She jumped into the back while everyone else took their seats. It was a tight fit with Chris driving and Bella in the front passenger seat, and two rows with Jillian and James, Nick, Matt, Aden, and Angie. They started down the long drive leaving the hotel. They drove to the end of town and through the old, covered bridge and turned a sharp right to start up the mountain. There was a lot of excited chatter about the previous night's investigation and what the day might bring. They planned to investigate the tunnels under the hotel later that night.

Chris had to take the drive slowly through the tight switchbacks and steep climbs winding up the mountain. As they continued the snow became deeper and the skies grew darker. Chris said, "We may need to stop before reaching the top if this truck cannot make it. Soon after he said this the truck tires started to spin, and Chris stopped and said this is where we walk. He turned the truck around so they could depart easily, and they all prepared for the hike.

They started the uphill hike with James reading the map as he walked. He said, "According to this map we are only about a quarter of a mile away from the line of trees." They walked through the snow and up the incline. Slippery at times, it helped to hold on to tree trunks and branches to keep from slipping and falling. They walked through the dense forest listening to the wind blowing through the trees. They reached the top of a hill and James announced they had arrived.

Standing in a small clearing about three-quarters of the way up the mountain they could clearly see the hotel and the town below. Looking up at the top of the mountain the trees became sparse until they disappeared. They were standing above the tree line Jillian and James were looking at from the hotel. Jillian and Bella walked over to the edge of the large rock to look over. It was covered with snow and very slick. Matt yelled to be careful and to stay away from the edge. It was a long fall. The rest of the group remained close by while surveying the area. Bella looked at Jillian and asked, "Do you see anything?" Jillian was tempted to walk a bit closer to the edge to get a better view. She leaned over and could see the tops of the trees, and she could see them moving. She assumed this was probably the wind. It was very dark and gray, and she continued to focus on one tree that seemed to be moving differently than the others. The branches were moving in different directions and not with the wind. She began to feel fear and dread. Familiar feelings these days.

Jillian took a small step toward the edge to get a better look. Bella was looking behind them watching and listening to the group discuss the easiest way to get closer to the line of trees. Suddenly they both heard a sickeningly loud cracking noise. In a split second, the chunk of rock Jillian was standing on started to give way. Everyone in the group heard the noise and turned to look. Bella screamed for Jillian to step toward her. Jillian froze, understanding her movement could break the rock altogether. She instinctively lowered herself close to the ground. She took a small wavering, shaky breath and crawled closer to Bella. James ran over to Bella and reached out his hand. They heard another loud crack. Jillian gasped and felt herself start to fall. James yelled, "Jillian!" Bella screamed as the rock moved down a few inches and stopped for a moment before completely breaking off. Jillian screamed and felt herself falling. She grabbed at anything she could find on the way down. She found and grabbed a bush branch, growing from the side of the cliff area. She grasped the branch first with one hand and then with the other. She was hanging from the bush dangling on the cliff scrambling to get a secure footing. James was yelling for her along with Bella, Chris, Matt, Nick, Aden, and Angie. She screamed back that she was ok, and she found a branch to hang on to. James yelled, "Can you pull yourself up?" She answered, "I am trying to pull myself up to a ledge above me."

She pulled and climbed her way up slowly and methodically. Her breathing was fast, her heart rate was high, and she could feel the adrenaline kick in. She finally found the edge and pulled herself up. She was stretched out on her stomach, gasping for breath, sweating, with tears in her eyes. She yelled, "I'm ok, I pulled myself onto this ledge." She stayed on the ground for a few moments catching her breath and slowly sat up. Chris said, "Hang on we will figure out a way to get to you!"

Jillian pulled herself together and looked around to see if there was a way to climb back up to where the group was. She turned around to look behind her and realized she was on a ledge next to the opening of a small cave. Looking out from the ledge she was closer to the tree line and had a lower and closer view of the trees. Her focus turned to the cave. She yelled to the group, "I found a cave!" Matt said, "Don't go in by yourself! It's too dangerous!" She stood looking into the cave, tempted to investigate but understanding she did not have the proper equipment and going by herself was not smart. Still, she found herself staring into the cave, unable to turn away. Did she just see movement? Did she just hear shuffling? The sinking feeling in her stomach returned. The fear and the dread were palpable. She walked closer taking slow, careful steps. Staring into the mouth of the cave, she jumped backward thinking she saw eyes. Red eyes looking back at her. She looked again and something was looking right back at her. A set of eyes, unblinking, staring at her from deep in the dark of the cave. Jillian screamed. Alarmed, the group yelled back asking if she was ok. "There is something in the cave, watching me!" She yelled. James knew something was very wrong. She was drawn to this location for a reason and now she was by herself facing an unknown threat.

The group turned to see Matt running back with climbing ropes. He found a way to climb down to the landing where Jillian was by taking a side way down. Matt always brought his climbing ropes, and everyone was so relieved that he did. They secured the rope and started climbing down one by one. It was not too challenging of a climb, and they made their way down quickly.

Jillian stood at the entrance of the cave, waiting for the group to climb down while staring back at the red eyes. It moved a step closer toward her. She stepped back aware she could not step back much farther without falling down the cliff again. She could barely breathe and started to cry. With no way to save herself, she had no options. Then she heard movement in the trees. She turned to look back at the trees and saw movement along the branches, and the trunks. Slithering movements that looked remarkably familiar. Dark figures with red eyes that could change shapes were slithering around on the tree limbs. She turned again toward the cave and the creature was moving closer to her. It was now near the light at the mouth of the cave. It hesitated in the shadows and Jillian could hear slow raspy breathing coming from the cave. The staring red eyes were growing larger, and she could see more detail as it remained in the shadows near the light. The outline of a dark shape became more in focus along with the eyes red with sloshing liquid that looked like blood. She saw a bright red foggy aura developing around this creature. She started to feel faint and realized she was holding her breath. At this moment she thought it was no coincidence that she was drawn to this location. Something wanted her here. It wanted to be seen. It wanted Jillian to see it, and feel the threat, the evil, and its significance. She felt surrounded by darkness and overwhelmed by a feeling of hopelessness and inevitability. Her eyes locked with its eyes. She felt paralyzed and could hear the movement all around her. She was suspended in a series of moments that felt like hours.

Then she heard the voices. Her friend's voices coming from the left, and before she found the strength to break the creature's gaze, it spoke to her. In a gravelly, deep, and raspy voice she heard it say, "Waiting... I have been waiting." The voice made her flinch, and this helped her to break away from its gaze. She heard feet hitting the ground and she turned quickly to see Matt running toward her with James close behind. Jillian fell to the ground exhausted and relieved to see everyone. James knelt next to her and noticed scratches on her face, and the shoulder wound had started bleeding again. For a moment Jillian forgot about the creature in the opening of the cave. She turned her head toward the mouth of the cave and the creature was gone. She no longer heard any movement in the trees behind her. They helped her to her feet and started the climb back up. When they were all back together where they started, Jillian told them what she saw.

The group stood listening intently. Aden walked over to the edge again, trying to get a look at the mouth of the cave. He was not able to see around the jutting rocks. He looked at the trees to see if he could spot anything moving. Straining his eyes, searching for anything unusual he was disappointed to find nothing. He had a feeling though. A dark, ominous feeling he could not shake. Aden shivered and walked back over to the group. Time had passed quickly, and it was now late in the afternoon.

James said, “We need to walk back to the car and reorganize at the Chateau.” They all agreed and started the walk back to the car, discussing everything they had experienced so far. Matt said, “I wonder if the tunnels we found leading from the Chateau lead all the way up here? Bella, who was walking close to Jillian held her arm as they walked. Jillian continued to look behind her. She could not shake off the shadow image of that creature. Mags was romping behind and around them as they walked, oblivious of the danger and the darkness.

Angie, who had been recently quiet spoke up. “I think this is one of the most haunted places we have ever experienced.” “I hope we are prepared for what we might experience tonight.” She felt overwhelmed by the entire area of Susurrous Pines. The town felt wrong and off. She wondered, “Could an entire town be haunted?” Aden said, “We could be in trouble here. Something feels familiar to me about this place. “I have never been here before and yet; I have a strong feeling of déjà vu everywhere we go.” He had an intense feeling something could go wrong tonight but he kept this to himself for now.

The group reached the truck and Mags jumped into the back while everyone got settled. The sun was beginning to set and soon it would be dark. Chris started the engine and made the drive back to the Chateau. They arrived back at the Chateau, unloaded the gear, and carried the gear up the front porch steps agreeing to meet back in the great entry hall in an hour to walk to town for dinner. They would plan out the evening at that time. One by one they slowly climbed the main staircase to the rooms.

Chapter 11

Revisiting The Past

Jillian sat on the bed with Mags sleeping next to her. James finished getting dressed and asked if she was ready to meet the group downstairs. She said, "I just need a bit more time." He nodded and left the room gently closing the door behind him. She glanced toward the window and noticed the dramatic colors of red, orange, and pink shining through. A beautiful sunset.

She placed her hand on Mag's back and felt the warm, soft fur between her fingers while watching her back slowly rising and falling as she took breaths in her peaceful sleep. Jillian stood up and walked over to the bathroom to wash her face with cold water. She looked at her tired face in the mirror. She had dark circles around her eyes, and the black eyeliner was starting to spread out under her eyes creating an even darker appearing ring. This investigation was taking a toll on her, and she could feel it. She cleaned the eyeliner from under her eyes and added fresh liner and lipstick, brushed her hair, and pulled it back. This helped her to feel a bit refreshed.

Jillian walked out of the bathroom and watched Mags jump up abruptly from a sound sleep and stand on the bed. As she continued to walk toward the bed, she could see Mags staring at the closet. Jillian looked at the closet and out of the corner of her eye, she caught a dark figure moving quickly from the closet to the door. It happened so quickly it appeared like a dark blurry mass. Mags whined, jumped to the floor, and ran to the door sniffing the area underneath the door frame. Jillian felt the fear kick as she felt compelled to check out the closet. She walked slowly and deliberately toward the closet with her heart pounding in her chest as she gasped for breath. Her hand was trembling as she slowly opened the closet door. When the door was open wide, she looked around inside. At first, she did not see anything amiss. As her eyes scanned the floor, she thought she noticed something in the back corner. She grabbed her phone and used the flashlight to focus on the back corner area. She gasped and jumped back when the light was directed at a dark smallish object leaning in the corner. Fear, dread, and astonishment struck her simultaneously as she pulled the small object out of the closet. Her hand trembling, she could not believe her eyes. Instantly she knew this was a warning.

Jillian grabbed her things, threw the object in a bag, and quickly left with Mags to join the others. She could not be alone in that room any longer. The door slammed behind them as they ran down the hall. Walking down the stairs she could feel the weakness in her legs. James watched her step down the stairs and noticed how pale she looked. He asked if everything was all right. Jillian said, "I am ok and will explain when we get to the diner." He accepted this while giving her an inquisitive and concerned look. She held his arm and put her head on his shoulder. She felt the weight of the additional item in her bag and could not shake the feeling of dread and the sense of doom. They sat at the bottom of the stairs waiting for Angie.

Angie stood looking out of the window of her room at the Chateau, watching the sun begin to set. The sun started the descent behind the mountains with brilliant orange, red and pink colors. The clouds and sky were glowing with all the assorted colors. The mountains were cast in dark shadows as the sunset progressed. Before she knew it, that beautiful sunset was over and now she could see the moon shining brightly.

It was time to meet the group downstairs and she was running late. Somehow, she found it difficult to move. Her feet were planted solidly on the ground, and she felt a hesitancy to go through with the investigation. Angie felt real concern and trepidation. Were they equipped to handle the level of evil she sensed in this town and the surrounding area? She did not possess any extraordinary gifts or talents to help them through the night. Only her knowledge of technology might help to catch tangible evidence on tape or video.

Angie walked to the bathroom, splashed water on her face, and brushed her hair. Without allowing herself to think about it anymore, she walked out of her room and shut the door behind her. She walked down the long hall to the top of the stairs and started down the staircase. She heard the familiar voices of the team and started to feel more at ease. They had been through so much together already and they would take care of one another. She could not consider the possibility that the darkness and evil might win. She shivered and shook off the doubt stepping down into the foyer with the group. She was greeted by Mags, and Angie leaned down to stroke her ears while Mags wagged her tail in approval.

With Angie's arrival, the team was complete, and they started the walk through the front door, across the porch, and down the front steps. They would plan the evening while eating dinner at the diner. They followed the long driveway from the Chateau to town. Mags was trotting along with them, sometimes stopping to sniff an interesting object before running to catch up. Jillian kept an eye on her to make sure she stayed close enough to the group.

The discussions were spirited as they walked and there was excitement in the air. Jillian stayed quiet and remained deep in her thoughts.

When they were settled in and comfortable at the diner and while they were eating, all eyes settled on Jillian. Everyone had noticed how quiet and brooding she had become. James asked her if she was ready to tell them what was going on. She looked up and said, "Something happened back at the Chateau. I need to tell you a story that takes me back to when I was very young." Jillian had the team's attention and she looked around at every person individually before she started.

I was in the second grade when my dad took me to the giant toy store. We were there to pick up a present for one of my friends. I felt euphoric and overwhelmed as we walked up and down the aisles looking at all the toys and games. I had never been to such a huge toy store with so many different toys in one place. My dad seemed happy as he watched me in such a joyful state. I held his hand and skipped happily down the aisles. I picked a toy I thought my friend would like and we stood in line to check out.

I looked around at the bins of toys and games around the checkout area. A bin of small bouncy balls, a bin of candy necklaces, another with yo-yos, and one with decks of cards. I walked over to a bin with a mix of different toys and picked through it. I discovered a dark-colored green, purple, brown, and black toy and picked it up. It was soft and almost gooey to the touch. It was slightly heavy and larger than my hand. A soft rubber monster attached to a stretchy looped string. I could hold the string and the dark green, purple, brown, and black colored rubber monster bounced around from the weight stretching out the string. I held the monster up to my nose and immediately moved it back and away from my face reacting to the strong rubber smell.

The monster was globular and had a face without detailed facial characteristics. It was quite scary to look at, yet I was drawn to it. I liked holding it and feeling the soft rubber. For some unknown reason, I needed to have it. It was a scary-looking globular rubber monster that smelled horrible, and I was drawn to it. Maybe it picked me. I felt compelled to ask my dad if I could have it. After all, it was in the sale bin and was less than $5. He looked at me strangely as I dangled this rubber monster from the string. He asked, "Why in the world do you want that strange-looking toy?" I told him I really liked it. He looked at the price, shrugged his shoulders, and agreed to buy it. I still do not understand what compelled me to want that rubber monster. I would reflect on this question over time.

On the drive home I spent more time inspecting the new toy. I started to get this uncomfortable feeling that I did not comprehend. Looking back, I would say I felt anxious, uncomfortable and for the first time I felt dread. Dread was a new feeling to me, and I did not understand it or know how to react.

I decided to embrace this new toy and thanked my dad for

buying it. I chose to always keep it with me to show how much I liked it. When I went to sleep that night, I placed it on my nightstand. This became the monster's place at bedtime-for a while at least.

The next day I woke up and decided to go biking. It was a warm, sunny, spring day. I called my neighborhood friends and we met outside with our bikes. There was a favorite hill that we enjoyed riding up and down. It was a long steep hill, and we could gain a lot of speed. Some kids became quite good at riding without touching the handlebars. Parents were always lecturing kids about how dangerous riding no-handed was, especially down the steep hill. I usually kept my hands on the handlebars just in case.

I was the youngest kid in my group of friends. Becky, Sasha, and Yvonne were my closest friends. Becky was usually the decision-maker in the group being the oldest. She was also incredibly creative. Looking back on my childhood, I was amazed at the creative games she would create. We used to create fantasy lands and would give tours. The themes would usually be from a movie, cartoon, or book. Becky would create a world of magic trees. The trees could grow unusual items like crayons, chalk, and markers. One of her favorites was the chalk tree. She would place chalk on branches and on the ground beneath a small seedling tree or bush and explain that it was a special chalk tree. I loved the chalk trees and for a while when I was very young, I believed they were real. It was a magical time for all of us.

On this nice warm spring day, we hopped on our bikes and pedaled to the top of the long hill. I had a green bike with a white seat and streamers hanging from the white handlebars. I placed my monster in the back pocket of my shorts. We took turns cruising down the hill and sometimes we would pedal hard at the top to give extra momentum.

I paused at the top of the hill waiting for Sasha to get a head start. I decided to pedal to gain momentum and then cruised down the hill faster and faster. I made it down the fastest part of the hill and as I was slowing down my front tire hit a large rock in the road. The front wheel turned, and my foot hit the ground hard. My shoe flew off and I found myself on the pavement under my bike. Everyone rushed over to see if I was ok. They lifted the bike off, and I sat up feeling dazed. I slowly stood up to evaluate my injuries. I had a skinned knee and then I looked down to see my bare foot sticking through my torn sock. My toes were bleeding. Then I started to feel the searing pain. Pain from the skinned knee that was bleeding and from my skinned toes. I felt my face turn red and the tears started to flow. I limped a block away to my house pushing my bike. When I returned home my mom bandaged me up. I would be stiff and sore for a number of days after that accident.

I went to sleep that night with throbbing knees and toes. As I drifted off to sleep, I looked at the globular monster sitting on my nightstand. I decided to name it Russ after a round and pudgy cat we once had. I thought naming the monster might help me to feel more comfortable with it. I was obsessively drawn to Russ. I needed to be near him. I did not feel happiness and excitement but mostly dread and anxiety when I thought about him, yet I felt compelled to keep him with me. I tried to ignore the negative feelings and push them away. I was too young to comprehend the complexity of what was happening.

The next morning, I woke up and dressed for school. I placed Russ in my backpack along with my books, binders, and lunch. It was going to be a busy day with softball practice after school. I left Russ in my backpack until the end of the day. I checked my backpack and noticed he had fallen to the bottom of the bag. I picked him up and placed him in the inner pocket of my jacket. That day was the only time I ever took a line drive to the head by the pitcher. The only time I was ever injured during a softball game. I ended up on the ground and had to be taken to urgent care. I spent the next couple of days in the dark with no screens to recover from a slight concussion. Russ stayed in place on my nightstand during my recovery. At this point, I was struggling with scared, negative feelings toward this toy that I did not like and yet I felt a dramatic attachment and a strange connection with it. I started to have serious concerns about my recent bad luck, accidents, and the possible connection to Russ.

At this point, I need to mention the nightmares. My extreme and vivid dream experiences started during this time. I would have intense, terrifying dreams about dark figures stalking me. These dark shapes would chase me through creepy forests at night, and they would haunt me in spooky houses. I would always be alone, and it felt like I was fighting for my life and my soul. I would wake up screaming and my parents would run into my room, all the while Russ was sitting on my nightstand as if he were watching. I never told my parents the detail about what took place in my dreams and why I was so scared. Somehow, I thought talking about the dreams and stating the details out loud might give the dreams more power. It was a horrifying time in my young life that I could never forget.

Then there was the incident with Robbie. Robbie was a kid who lived around the corner and would often join us when we rode our bikes down the hill, and around the neighborhood. He was what I would call a bossy boy, who had a bit of a mean streak.

We all met one day and decided to ride up and down the big hill. It was the usual group of girls and Robbie. The other girls went first, and one by one they flew down the hill on bikes. Robbie and I were left waiting at the top of the hill for our turn. While we waited, he noticed Russ hanging out of my pocket. He grabbed the string to see what it was. He looked carefully at Russ the monster, placed him in his pocket, and took off on his bike down the hill. I did not have time to react and just yelled, "Hey, that is mine!" He was riding extremely fast, and the other girls were waiting off to the side of the road at the bottom of the hill watching.

I watched in horror as he started to lose control. His bike swerved and flipped over in the air. Robbie landed hard, face down on the pavement, and was motionless. I rode my bike down to where he fell while the other girls threw down their bikes and ran over to see if he was ok. Robbie remained motionless and when I approached, I found Russ on the pavement next to him. I felt a chill go down my spine. A neighbor who had been standing in a nearby front yard and witnessed the accident called emergency services.

Robbie lived, but he had a broken collarbone, and a concussion, and was in the hospital for many days. I was convinced from that day forward that Russ was evil. Terrible things happened to the person who possessed him. I realized I needed to get rid of Russ. That ended up being the biggest challenge. Every time I hid Russ, or tried to throw him away, he would show up again that very night. He would be in the usual place on my nightstand as if nothing were different. It did not make sense. I did not think anyone would believe me if I told them about my experiences. Russ terrorized me for weeks. Finally, I found an old safe and asked my dad if I could use it. I secretly locked Russ in the safe and kept the safe in the basement hidden away. After I locked Russ in the safe, my nightmares stopped and over time I was able to distance myself from the experience and return to my regular, less eventful life. But I never forgot. I could never forget.

When my parent's house was sold, I took that safe and hid it in a place only I know about.

The team was so engaged with the story Jillian was telling, that they stopped eating. They had been hanging on every word. Bella spoke up and said, "That is a terrifying and disturbing story. I am so sorry you went through that difficult time. Toys should be fun and leave pleasant memories. But why are you telling us this story now?"

Jillian slowly reached into her bag and pulled out a rubber globular object with an old, yellowed string. She said, "I found this in the back corner of the closet in our room at the Chateau after seeing a large dark, misty mass appear in the room. She opened her hand to show the dark rubber, globular monster. This is Russ...

She placed Russ on the table, and everyone froze. Jillian said, "I believe this is a message and a warning. The evil we are dealing with, it has access to our deepest inner thoughts and experiences. It knows what we are afraid of. It wants us to understand the power it possesses. The power is real, and it is invasive."

Nick looked at her and said, "You need to find a safe place for that." Jillian said, "I plan to lock it up in a container I have in my car for now." In silence, they all finished eating. Each member of the team sat nervously thinking about past experiences, fears, and vulnerabilities they carried with them. They thought about how these past events and experiences might be used against them. Eventually, Aden spoke up and said, "It is not just our scariest, darkest thoughts and experiences. This evil, this scourge has access to what we do not remember. Experiences so terrible our minds prevent us and protect us from remembering."

Bella looked at Aden thoughtfully while he was speaking. He looked nervous and afraid. She understood the difficult childhood he had shared with the team. When he was young, and his family lived in an old house. That house is where he had many haunting experiences. He always felt different than other kids his age. He grew out of toys earlier than kids he knew and was much more interested in reading. He would usually lose interest in conversations with kids and felt the age-appropriate subject matter was boring. His parents eventually had him tested and realized he was very smart. They placed him in a special school that was more challenging for him. He had two older sisters and they never had any unusual experiences in the home.

His experiences started out small. He would see something move out of the corner of his eye behind a door, or in the corner of a room. He would hear footsteps behind him as he moved around the house, especially at night. This would always terrify him. He felt as if he was being watched all the time when in the house. Then he started hearing voices. It sounded like people talking when he knew no one else was in the house. He could never understand what was being said, but he could hear discussions going on. His family never believed him, so he stopped telling them. He felt alone and targeted by whatever was in the house. Then the sleepwalking started. The sleepwalking experiences, or whatever it was, alarmed him the most. He would wake up in various parts of the house with no memory of how he got there. He would sometimes wake up outside. It could be raining or freezing cold, and he would be outside. Aden remembered one night when he woke up outside and had to ring the doorbell to be let back into the house. His family thought he walked out the front door and locked it before shutting the door. All while he was sleeping.

They took him to sleep specialists and counselors. They tried different medications, but nothing really helped. He developed anxiety around bedtime. He feared sleep and what it might bring. This continued for years until they moved out of the house when his father got a new job. When they moved everything stopped. He never had another sleepwalking experience until the Edin house investigation. The Edin house investigation brought his past back for him to face in ways he could never have imagined. Angie also wondered if there was more to his childhood experiences that he has not shared. Angie looked at Aden now, sitting across from her and she could see that scared kid. He had worry lines across his forehead and looked very tired. She wondered if he should participate in the cave exploration they had planned for this evening.

Jillian picked up Russ and placed him back in her bag. There was no explanation for how this toy showed up in her closet after being locked away in a secret place for so many years. She felt anxious just being in the presence of Russ. She needed to get it back to her car as soon as possible.

Her eyes wandered back over to the bulletin board with the community messages on it. Standing up, she walked over to look at the bulletin board again. This time, she noticed different notices on the bulletin board. Copies of old newspaper articles.

One article covered the history of the mines including the explosion incident that killed so many people. This article listed the names and ages of all the people killed. She looked more closely at the list and counted the number of children who died. Thirty-six workers died that day including ten children and one woman. It was an astounding number of people. The authorities never discovered the cause of the accident. Jillian continued to scan the bulletin board and found a number of articles about people who had gone missing when hiking in the nearby mountains. In addition, she found articles on the bulletin board about hikers reporting unusual sightings. Sightings involving ghostly figures, signs of witchcraft practices, and unidentified noises in the forests. These articles supported the findings by the Barrington brothers, as well as the research Jillian and James had done on the area surrounding Susurrous Pines. The article about Flannery Token and the funeral services was still on the bulletin board. She found another article about the woman who died in the mining accident. It turns out this woman was a relative of the Luster family and had gone to the mines to bring food to the workers. She was known as a kind woman whose family, like so many in Susurrous Pines during that period had fallen on tough times. She was married to one of the miners, and they had three children working in the mines. The entire family was killed in the accident. Jillian wondered why the articles on the bulletin board were different than before. They were still very old but simply different. The woman working at the diner looked at her and as if she knew what Jillian was thinking, she said, "We like to post different articles that are about the history of the town. The townspeople who have lived here and called Susurrous Pines home always appreciate this. We never forget." The way this woman spoke, it was like she was having regular communication with people who had died. Jillian asked her, "What do you mean they appreciate this?" The woman looked at her and said, "It has always been this way in Susurrous Pines." She turned and walked into the back behind the kitchen area. The people here are very mysterious, Jillian thought as she walked back over to the table.

Back at the table, she announced to the team, "You all should go check out the bulletin board." They silently stood up and walked over to look at the board. Each article was passed around and read before placing it back on the board. The team had a lot to talk about on the walk back to the Chateau. Aden remained quiet and withdrawn. They agreed to meet at the entrance of the hotel after taking a couple of hours to relax. The plan for the night was to explore the tunnels leading from the Chateau.

They all separated and went to their rooms. Mags led the way leaping up the long staircase. Aden, Nick, and Matt walked down the long hall, and each opened the door to their rooms. Matt said, "See you in a couple of hours."

Jillian opened the door and fell on the bed sighing heavily. She locked Russ in the box in her car, but the darkness had already infiltrated her thoughts. The warning felt very ominous.

Chapter 12

The Source and The Power

Aden found he was unable to stop pacing around his room. He was uneasy, scared, and felt vulnerable. Familiar feelings he could not shake off. Since pacing was not helping, he moved to the bed in another attempt to calm down. This investigation had uncovered parts of his past that he had not thought about in many years. He was deciding whether he should continue the investigation based on a nagging thought that there was something he was not remembering about his childhood experiences. Something important, that might jeopardize the entire investigation and place everyone at risk, especially him.

He took out his phone and searched for old photographs of when he was young, during that challenging time. He found a few photos and while studying the first photo, noticed how innocent he looked standing in front of his house carrying a baseball bat and mitt going to practice. While looking at the few old photos on his phone, he stopped at the picture of him sitting on the porch in a chair with the family dog. He had fond memories of that dog and felt a bit sad as he remembered. While looking at this photo he suddenly felt his stomach drop. He enlarged the photo on his phone to see more detail. In plain view, he could see a dark mass standing behind him in the photo. He began to feel sick as he continued to look at this photo. The dark figure behind him did not look human. It was crouched over with long arms and legs. It was holding its arms away from its body in a threatening posture behind him as he was sitting in the chair. He could not see detailed facial characteristics except for the eyes. The dark figure was holding its long bony arms out in a way that made it appear like it was planning to strangle him. The red eyes were staring directly at him through the photograph. Aden began to shake and dropped his phone. He jumped when there was a knock at his door.

Angie stopped by to see if he was ok. He invited her in, and they sat on the bed. She immediately noticed how pale he looked. His long dark hair fell over in front of his face as he looked down. Angie had always felt drawn toward Aden. He had a sweet and gentle way about him. She thought he had a sensitive face and walked around with a thoughtful expression that showed vulnerability. She found herself feeling protective of him. He was quite different than she was. She always had a reputation for being very blunt and matter of fact with her communications. She was told she came across as abrasive and overconfident at times. Angie had kept a small group of friends over an extended period of time. She typically had trouble getting close to people and it took a long time for her to trust others and let them in her bubble. As she sat with Aden, she thought about how it was different with him. She could talk with him and have deep conversations without any concern about trust. She was instantly comfortable with him. Now she sat next to him on the bed feeling worried. They sat quietly for a few minutes.

Aden spoke up and began to tell her his concerns regarding the investigation and the ominous feelings he had about his past. Then he told her about the photo. Angie asked, "Can I see the photo?" He picked up the phone, pulled up the photo again, and after enlarging it he handed the phone to her. He could see fear and concern on her face as she viewed the photo. She asked, "Have you ever noticed this figure in the photo before?" He answered, "No, never." Angie said, "Let's bring this to the others and see what they say. Then she asked to see the additional old photos he had on his phone. She looked at the photo of him standing in front of his house with the baseball bat and glove. Her eyes grew large as she enlarged that photo. She asked, "Have you ever noticed this?" He took the phone from her and gasped. He could see two dark figures crouched over behind him peering around one of the columns on the front porch. They had similar long arms and legs and the red eyes. They were partially hidden by the column. He felt his breathing get faster and started to break out in a sweat. Angie said, "We need to arrange an early meeting with the group and show them these photos. She contacted everyone and they met in the hallway outside the rooms.

Angie and Aden explained what was happening and they handed the photos around for everyone to look at. Jillian said, "I believe this is another warning." Bella said, "That is terrifying." Bella felt a shiver as she remembered the creatures from the previous Edin house investigation. She pushed the memories away understanding she could scare herself to the point of not being able to participate any further. Chris, Matt, and Nick viewed the photos with fear in their eyes. Jillian looked at Aden and asked, "Do you think you can go through with the investigation tonight?" He said he was not sure and was concerned about placing everyone at risk. There was also concern about the Edin house investigation and how that impacted him. Matt spoke up and said, "We are here for you and respect whatever decision you make." Aden looked down at his shoes while he took a moment to decide. In an instant, he decided to move ahead and participate. He thought about the possibility of finding answers to what happened to him and the need to find answers outweighed the need to protect himself and stay safe. The struggles he had experienced over the years related to his childhood experiences had been significant. Maybe with answers, he could make peace with it. The team knew Aden well and they were with him during the Edin house investigation. Aden was not sure why the Susurrous Pines investigation felt so different. So much more inherently dangerous. They fully understood the risks…or did they? The team was supportive and warmly accepted his decision. Matt said as he patted his shoulder, "Aden, I understand how difficult this situation is for you and I respect your decision to stay with us. Please let us know if at any time you need to change your mind and opt-out." They all went back to the rooms to get ready for the evening and prepare for the tunnel investigation.

Jillian was stretched out on the bed again with Mags in

her lap. They had about an hour before the tunnel exploration investigation was starting. She found herself thinking about Aden. His experiences as a child, the vulnerability, and challenges he faced during the Edin house investigation. The way dark spirits had the ability to take over his body and influence him at times. She revisited the possibility that Aden has powerful, specific, and extraordinary gifts that he does not fully understand. Abilities he has not learned how to use. Maybe his abilities to connect with spirits were being used against him now because he has not learned how to use these gifts to his advantage. The vulnerability and risk could be not understanding how to protect himself. If he could develop these abilities and learn how to protect himself while using them, maybe he could be a more powerful asset in this battle against evil. It was a dangerous thought and knowing how to help Aden with potentially dangerous and untapped power could open all of the team members up to risks they might not be prepared for. She would need to talk with Chris about it. Chris might have more insight on the matter.

Overall, she felt a renewed energy. As overwhelming as the experience so far had been, she was anticipating discovery and the more information uncovered meant they would find a way to beat back the evil that was once again trying to infiltrate their world.

Then she remembered the spell books they found. So much had happened she forgot about William Luster's spell books! She grabbed the bag stored under the bed and took out the books. Jillian began to quickly go through the books. There were spells that might help them, and she decided to bring the books with her to the tunnels that evening.

Jillian waited for James who went downstairs to find snacks for later that night. She felt herself becoming drowsy and closed her eyes. Mags was breathing softly in her sleep cuddled up next to her. Jillian shifted her position on the bed to avoid pressure on her shoulder area which was still very sore and painful. She let out a long breath and fell asleep.

She was walking through a tunnel of bright light. At first, she could not see anything clearly. Just brilliant bright light reflecting all around her. As she continued to walk, she looked to her right and she could see two small children crying, holding hands, and walking together through the bright light. She recognized this scene, although she was not sure why this was familiar. Then she looked closely at the faces of the young children. It was Jillian and James when they were very young. They were walking through the portal their mothers created during that fierce battle between good and evil. Both of their mothers died during that battle so many years ago and Jillian and James survived by walking through that portal into the current time. Now she was standing with young Jillian and James in that portal and observing them through her dream.

The two of them continued walking through the long tunnel of light while crying and holding hands. The sounds of little children crying brought tears to Jillian's eyes. The fear they must have felt. Watching, she suddenly became aware of another presence with them. She frantically looked around, feeling the familiar dread and fear. A strong sensation of losing her stomach, like going down a big hill on a roller coaster- was overwhelming. She felt her legs weakening and bent her legs to stay standing. A heavy darkness wrapped around Jillian when she heard a voice say, "I am here." "I have always been here." The voice was raspy, screechy, and sounded like speech within a growl. Jillian stopped and looked around for the source of the voice. She watched the young Jillian and James continue the walk until it became too steep for them, and they began to fall. She could hear the loud and desperate screams. Suddenly two long, thin, bony, gray arms with paper-thin loose skin hanging like torn fabric, and thin extended, bony fingers with long yellowed fingernails reached out and grabbed the kids by the arms. The creature had a bright red aura that was growing. The red liquid was dripping around it and dripping onto the kids. They were helpless and hanging, unable to break free. They looked shocked and confused and this creature said, "You will not get away, I will find you again." "Always remember I am watching and waiting." The creature spoke in that raspy growling voice and Jillian covered her ears. She now remembered. As she watched, the creature lost its grip as both Jillian and James struggled wildly to break free. It dropped young Jillian and James and they fell into the forest far below. The portal closed and the creature shrieked in protest as it slowly turned to look at Jillian. She gasped looking directly at those red eyes with the blood swishing inside the dark sockets. The eyes were deep-set in the gray skull-like sunken face, with wispy long white hair blowing. It said, "It is time." "I have been waiting."

Jillian woke up with James shaking her and Mags standing in front of her face whining. He said as he helped her to sit up, "You have been having a nightmare and I had great difficulty waking you up." She looked at him feeling groggy and shaky. She took a few moments to gather her thoughts. He sat next to her waiting to hear about the dream. The team knocked on the door and James let them in before returning to sit next to Jillian. They were late to the team meeting place, and the team came looking for them. They all looked concerned standing around the bed. Jillian looked at James while holding his hand and said, "When we were very young, and we walked through that portal to the present time, we were not alone. Creatures, dark spirits, whatever we call them, were there with us. Similar creatures like what I saw in the cave, in the car at the car accident, in the dream when my shoulder was injured, and like the creatures, we saw throughout the Edin house investigation. I believe we were touched somehow by these creatures when we passed through that portal. They have a deep connection to us. We passed through the portal and through the dimension where they reside, and this helped to create more of an awareness of our world. They watched us leave the portal so many years ago, and because of this, we helped to create the awareness and the opportunity for them to enter our world. I believe when we closed the portal during the Edin house investigation, they found another entrance here in Susurrous Pines. There are many reasons the dark spirits are attracted to this place. There were spirits in a state of unrest here and they were waiting. I have a sense that the spirits here suffered trauma, unexpected and violent deaths, torment, and sadness in Susurrous Pines. They had unfinished business and they are angry. They have been stuck and waiting for an exceedingly long time."

James looked concerned and took his free hand to nervously play with his hair as he said, "I believe that when spirits are not at rest and have unfinished business as you say, the strong human feelings of anger, sadness, loss, betrayal from life, and confusion due to violent unexpected death, eventually over time leads them to become something else. They begin to lose their humanity and are overtaken by the anger and these strong negative emotions. This is how true evil can be created. Empathy, sympathy, compassion, sensitivity, the ability to love, these experiences that make us human-all of this is lost. They become dangerous and powerful beings vulnerable to evil manipulation. When stronger, more powerful creatures or dark spirits find them, like the dark spirit that used to be William Luster-they easily and willingly become part of the evil scourge. It allows powerful spirits to develop an army."

Jillian sat up straight and looked directly at James and said, "There is something else though. I believe there are benevolent spirits present in that same dimensional space. Spirits that have not been able to move on and are stuck but for different reasons. They may feel an attachment to the living, or to a space or structure that was meaningful to them when they were living. They may not be ready to let go or have not accepted that they have died. These spirits are also waiting to enter back into our world, but for different reasons. Not to harm but to help. They can resist the evil at least for a time and could be our allies."

Angie asked, "If the evil, dark spirits, or creatures can show themselves to us they are escaping into our world already. Why can't they just use what power they have to take over? What is preventing them from infiltrating our world now?" Chris spoke up and said, “It takes a lot of energy and power to break through into our world. Even if a portal is open, it will drain energy and power from a spirit when moving in and out of the portal. These dark spirits or creatures spend years trying to gain enough power to enable them to move through a portal. They remain where the evil force is strong. They can stay connected to a place for years, decades, and even centuries. While there, they can gather and join with other evil forces and spirits to gain momentum and power. It develops into a formidable force that becomes the scourge.” “We experienced the beginning of this at the Edin house investigation. We were able to fight back and close the portal.” Chris, followed up by saying, “I have read this information in the ancestral books my family has kept for centuries. These books contain information about the possibilities and the worst-case scenarios. I was hoping these were just hypotheticals and intended for training and preparation and not realistic outcomes in our real world. Now I think we are seeing the truth.”

Everyone in the room contemplated what was said. It was a thoughtful quiet that took over for a few minutes. Chris spoke up and said, “As integrals, you already have extraordinary gifts connecting you to the spirit world. The experience you both had walking through that portal, and the contact you had with the spirits at such an early age will make it easier for the spirits to find you in our world. They may be able to sense you and seek you out. This is both helpful to us and extremely dangerous. This may be why Jillian’s dreams are so powerful, and why James can see so deeply when he touches objects. I have wondered about the close connection you have with one another and how this influences your abilities individually as well as when you use them simultaneously. I have had concerns about the potential for this connection to create additional danger for both of you. It is something for you to be aware of. I believe this deep connection is the reason why when Jillian and James are angry with one another this directed anger can cause physical harm to them. There is extra power and strength there. You both may also have additional abilities yet to be discovered."

Chris was very respected by the group, and they listened intently. When he was finished, Jillian and James looked at each other knowingly. They were beginning to understand the complexity of the situation for them personally. Jillian trusted Chris implicitly however he did not always share everything with them. If he intentionally left out information, she understood it would be in a sincere effort to protect them and help keep them safe. She had always been a person who enjoys learning as much information as possible. She lives by the philosophy that knowledge is power, and knowledge can empower a person to make educated decisions. It could help a person feeling out of control in a situation to take control all through research and learning pertinent information. She was now forced to trust Chris to make decisions about sharing information with them that might help them make different choices- changing possible outcomes. This was a vulnerable experience for her that made her uneasy. James squeezed her hand reassuringly as if he understood exactly what she was thinking about. She squeezed his hand back and they stood up with the others to start preparing for the night.

Jillian and James moved around the room gathering gear together to start the tunnel exploration. As she was gathering her gear she said, "I believe Flannery Token is a benevolent spirit. He may be able to help us." "I have sensed his spirit around us ever since we saw him in that museum. He seems to be a kind soul who has a strong connection to Susurrous Pines and clearly has learned how to move between worlds. I have a sense that he wants to help us." Bella spoke up as she walked toward the door and said, "I have sensed this spirit also. I believe he wants to help however he is not always able to move into our world. He is held back at times. The evil tries to suppress him and turn him. Flannery Token has had the strength so far to resist and break away from this hold. His strength comes from his strong love and passion for Susurrous Pines. His ability to overcome the temptation and power of the evil side is only temporary. He is in danger just like the rest of us"

Chapter 13

The Tunnels

The group walked to the meeting place at the foyer of the Chateau. The mood was mixed with Matt and Nick feeling energized to see what the night would bring. Angie, Aden, Jillian, James, Bella, and Chris were all feeling uneasy. They were approaching the tunnel exploration with dread.

They brought extra gear including ropes, and flashlights, with a store of batteries. To prevent them from getting lost, special brightly colored lighted tubes were brought to use as markers. They could place these markers strategically on the floors, the walls, or wherever made sense at the time, to mark the way back if the tunnels turned out to be as long and winding as they predicted. The team brought extra water and snacks preparing for a long night.

They stood together and Chris asked, "Is everyone ready to go?" They all nodded in agreement and made the way up the first flight of stairs to the attic. The Chateau was especially dimly lit on this night, and they could barely see where they stepped. The sound of the wind whipping through the pines made a stirring, sweeping sound with the sudden gusts, and a soft whispering sound as it slowed down. The wind was louder as they continued to climb the stairs and reached higher elevations. The old house seemed to rattle and creak as the wind hit the exterior.

Once in the attic they opened the door in the wall and prepared to descend all the way down one by one to the lower level. They were bringing video cameras and would use phone videos, along with walkies, and voice recorders. It took about ten minutes for all of them to get to the bottom level and clear the stairs.

They placed flashlights in the small space near the stairs while they quietly organized the gear. Matt walked to the far end of the room to find the exit to the tunnel. It was dark damp and musty. There was a smell that Jillian did not notice before. A strange, putrid, horrible smell that stung their noses and throats. Bella and Nick were complaining about the smell and coughing a bit. Aden stood looking at the drawings of the hooded figure. He focused his flashlight on the final drawing of the creature, shivered, and said, “These are very creepy drawings.” Angie put her hand on his shoulder to comfort him. Chris cleared his throat and called out to Matt. Matt answered but his voice sounded far away. Chris used the walkie to try to contact Matt. He answered right away and said he had just walked down the tunnel a short distance and was on his way back.

The group walked toward the tunnel entrance and could see Matt’s flashlight getting brighter as he moved closer to them. He met up with them and was extremely excited. He said, “I found a split off further down. There are three tunnel options to follow. We can split up and take different tunnels while staying connected with our walkies.” Bella walked toward him and asked, “Shouldn't we stay together? Is it safe to separate?” Aden said, “As long as we stay connected and are in small groups, I think it's all right. We can cover more ground this way.” Chris sighed and said “I think it makes sense to split up and explore all three tunnels at the same time. Jillian, James, and Nick can take the first tunnel. Matt, Aden, and Angie can take the second tunnel, and Bella and I will take the last tunnel. Everyone keeps walkies on at all times. We need to stay connected regularly. Bring your markers in case the tunnels branch out more and become more complex. We do not want to get lost. Keep track and keep a record of where you are going.

It was time for them to start the exploration. They all did a quick gear check and assembled in front of the tunnel they were going to explore. There was nervous energy in the air. They stood looking at one another in the dark with the only illumination created by the flashlights. Matt said, “Be safe everyone.” They all nodded and started down the tunnels. The sound of footsteps and shuffling could be heard from the three tunnels. The spaces were narrow and occasionally they had to step over rock debris that had fallen from the ceiling or the walls.

Jillian, James, and Nick made their way through the narrow and winding tunnel. The sound from the footsteps was loud as the shuffling noise echoed and bounced off the stone. Jillian kept glancing behind them. They were illuminating the tunnel ahead and it was completely pitch dark behind them. It made her nervous and on edge. Nick was the last one and he saw her glancing behind them. He said, "Please don't tell me you see something behind me." She laughed and responded, "Don't worry you will know if I see something behind us." He scoffed sarcastically as they continued. The tunnel seemed exceptionally long. James asked, "How far do you think this goes?" They were all beginning to feel isolated and somewhat claustrophobic the deeper in they walked. Darkness surrounded them.

They continued walking, speaking softly as they went. Jillian asked, "Do you notice our voices sound different suddenly?" The echo sound from the voices seemed to be opening up like they were moving toward more of an open space. They picked up the pace and James used his flashlight to try to see more of what was ahead of them. He could see they were moving toward an opening in the tunnel. They reached the opening and walked through and into a large room. There were tunnel offshoots from this room. They walked around the room looking into every edge and alcove and studying the walls and high stone ceiling. On the far side, they found what appeared to be an old pedestal or pulpit with a table next to it. There were markings on the walls and the floor consistent with devil worship and witchcraft practices. A large pentagram was drawn on the floor with dusty remains of what appeared to be candle wax and the remnants of candles that had burned located around the drawing. They gathered around this area studying the markings and looking at the tables. The only sounds they could hear were the sounds made by their own footsteps. Walking, shuffling, and scraping noises as they moved around the large room.

James used his walkie to check in with the others. Matt and Chris answered and said they were still walking through the tunnels. James told them what they found. Matt asked him to make sure to take photos and video. Jillian, James, and Nick spent the next few minutes taking videos and photos. Jillian was taking photos of the table and noticed what looked like dried drips of blood. She mentioned this while she continued to take photos. Nick and James walked over to take a look. Everything was covered with a layer of dust and as Jillian cleared off the dust with her hand, they could see dried drips of a dark red liquid covering the table. She asked, "I wonder if this is where William Luster practiced witchcraft and spells?" She remembered the spell books and took them out of her bag. The spell book and the curse book were placed on the table, and this caused a cloud of dust to float into the air. The three of them leaned over the table to look at the books.

Jillian opened the curse book and was immediately fascinated. There were so many curse choices. Then she noticed the notes in the margins. She assumed these books were William Luster's and that he put his own notes in the margins. It was written in a messy script, but she could make out some of the words. It looked like he created his own versions of the curse spells. The notes showed different edited instructions. The book read like a recipe book with the included steps of incantations. They read with the focused light of the flashlights surrounded by darkness. Nick opened the spell book and again found the script in the margins with edits to the instructions for each spell. It appeared the spell book could work along with the curse book. Certain spells could be antidotes for specific curses and vice versa. Jillian looked specifically for a spell to close a portal or door. As she did this, she heard a loud bang coming from behind her in the back of the room. They all jumped and looked behind them. There was nothing there to explain the noise. It was quiet again and they nervously turned back to the books.

Jillian held on to the edge of the table and incidentally

felt something underneath. She took her flashlight and looked underneath the table. She found a hidden drawer. Nick and James looked underneath and tried to open the drawer. It was locked and they could see a keyhole. Jillian wondered, "What could be in that drawer?" James stood up and said, "I wonder where the key might be." Nick commented, "There is no telling. It has been so long since anyone has been down here." Suddenly they jumped again, startled after hearing another sound in the back of the room. All three used the flashlights and scanned the back area walls, and floor. As she moved her flashlight around the room, Jillian saw a black shadow quickly moving on the wall. She could not follow it because it was moving so fast. She screamed and Nick and James huddled with her in the middle of the room as they were also watching movement on and along the walls. "What is that?" Jillian asked in a panicked voice. Nick said, "We are sitting ducks in here." James looked for the other tunnel access points. They could hear shuffling and movement all around them. James said, "We can either go back the way we came, or we can choose another tunnel." He turned to look at the tunnel access they took to get to this room. He realized the movement was all around that area. Dark shapes that were changing and morphing as they were crawling on the floor, walls, and ceiling. The dark shadows were moving closer to them as they stood together in the middle of the room. James watched as these shadows surrounded the tunnel opening that would bring them back to the staircase room where they started. He looked at the other tunnel entrances and said, "We need to choose another tunnel. We cannot go back the way we came." They started to run toward the closest tunnel as the dark figures were getting closer. They ran as fast as they could go with only light from the flashlights. Jillian yelled, "Be careful, we don't have enough light to be running through the tunnels this way." They were panicked, breathing hard and running so fast they did not look back to see what might be following them. Nick slowed down to shine his light behind him. He did not see the shadow figures anymore. He yelled ahead to Jillian and James, "Slow down they don't seem to be following us anymore." They slowed down to a fast walk, as they tried to calm down.

Matt, Aden, and Angie walked slowly and carefully through the tunnel. It was winding with many turns, and they found themselves walking up steep inclines. Going down the other side of these inclines was even more precarious in the dark. Matt walked along looking down at the ground and said, "I have never walked through a tunnel/cave area like this with so many steep hills. We must be walking up one of the mountains." The ceiling was low and when walking up a steep incline the ceiling was so low Matt and Aden had to stoop over and protect their heads. The low ceiling made the space feel much more claustrophobic. After walking for about 20 minutes Matt stopped abruptly. Angie bumped into Matt and Aden bumped into Angie. Matt said," check this out, we need to make a choice." They were looking at other tunnel offshoots. One tunnel continued on an incline, and the other appeared to go down. Aden spoke softly and said, "Let's continue going up. If we believe this is leading us up the mountain let's see where it goes." Matt took out the markers they brought and placed them on the floor and on the wall. They proceeded through the new tunnel.

The space became even more narrow and smaller as they walked, and they felt very cramped. Aden started to feel even more uncomfortable. It was extremely quiet except for their own shuffling and footsteps on the stone floor. Matt kicked a loose stone on the floor and felt more stones crunching underneath his shoes. Angie said, "The floor seems different. The stones are loose." Matt stopped short again. They all pointed flashlights ahead of where Matt stood. They were looking at a pile of rocks and rubble blocking the tunnel in front of them. Matt exclaimed, "This tunnel system is unstable. This is dangerous. We need to turn around and backtrack." As they turned around, a loud bang occurred, originating from the other side of the pile of rubble. They could hear shuffling and what sounded like mumbling and growling. They all paused for a moment to listen. They could hear whispering now, along with the mumbling and growling. Suddenly a loud, bone-chilling shriek came from the other side of the pile of rocks and rubble. Angie screamed and took off running. Matt and Aden followed close behind. They ran all the way back to where they found the offshoots and quickly took the other tunnel. They stopped running a few minutes later when it was determined nothing was following them. Angie was out of breath; Matt could barely speak, and Aden remained noticeably quiet and shaky.

Angie, Matt, and Aden quickly walked this time as they made progress through the tunnel. The space was very narrow, and they were walking downhill. A short time later they came across a number of tunnel offshoots on the right and left sides. Matt stopped again and they all flashed lights down each offshoot. Angie spoke up and said, "How do we know what way to choose? This is becoming a labyrinth." They continued to move forward without taking a new tunnel and observed what appeared to be endless offshoots from this tunnel. Angie glanced back to see Aden following behind her at a distance. He was walking slowly and shining his light down each offshoot as he walked past. He seemed very preoccupied. She asked him, "Aden are you all right? You don't seem like yourself." He looked up and said in a very faint voice, "Do you hear it? Do you hear the noises in the other tunnels?" She stopped and listened. She answered, "No, I don't hear anything right now." He seemed discouraged she could not hear the noises. She asked, "What do you hear?" Aden walked closer to her and whispered in her ear, "I can hear movement, shuffling, footsteps, and deep voices whispering. I cannot make out what they are saying." By now Matt had joined them to find out what was holding them up. He was listening to the conversation. Matt could not hear the noises either. Aden was clearly shaken up as they all were at this point. Maybe his imagination was working overtime. They were deep into the tunnels at this point. It was dark and creepy, and they definitely heard beings or something moving around on the other side of that pile of rubble and rocks. It was understood they were not alone.

Angie asked Aden and Matt, "Should we take one of these tunnels to see if we can find what is creating the noise Aden is hearing?" Matt said, "If we take too many turns, we increase our chances of getting lost. We were running when we took this tunnel and did not leave markers. I am keeping written track of where we have gone so far, but the darkness and vastness of these tunnels will make it more difficult to find our way back. He contacted James via his walkie. James reported what they found so far. The large room with the table and the drawer, and the pulpit. The area that appeared to be a place where rituals were practiced. James reported the three of them were chased out of the room by shadow figures when they were looking for a way to open the drawer. Matt reported what happened when they encountered the pile of rocks blocking off the tunnel and what they heard on the other side. He also spoke about the sounds Aden heard and the extensive tunnel system discovered. Chris and Bella were quietly listening. So far, they had encountered nothing unusual and were continuing down the same tunnel originally entered.

For now, Matt, Angie, and Aden decided not to stray from the current path forward and stayed in the same tunnel. They continued to pass numerous tunnel offshoots along the way.

James, Jillian, and Nick walked taking each step with purpose while listening to the sounds of the footsteps echoing. Jillian whispered, "It seems like we are being herded by these spirits in a specific direction. Matt, Aden, and Angie were also forced to go in a certain direction. I wonder if we are being led into a trap." Nick stated, "I have that same feeling and I hope we are not correct. We have come this far and want to find answers to help us protect ourselves and others from evil. Taking chances is the only way." Jillian listened and realized how committed Nick and the team were to the mission. She felt grateful and honored to be connected and working with such sincere and honest team members and friends.

After about 10 more minutes of walking, James stopped. He said, "I see an opening up ahead." He walked toward the large opening at the end of the tunnel and pointed his flashlight around to check out the space before entering. He said, "It looks ok." They all took a breath and stepped together into a huge open space.

They stood using flashlights to take it all in. It was a large, cavernous space. The slightest noise made was magnified by the surrounding stone creating loud echoes.

Vast, soaring ceilings created an overwhelming feeling as they stood in the middle of this enormous space. Cave rock formations in various shapes, sizes, and colors were visible. Stalactites and stalagmites were growing from the ceiling and the floor throughout the space. Sparkles from the various stones reflected in the light as they scanned the space with the flashlights. Dripping noises from water flowing down through the ceiling of the cave echoed loudly. The flashlights as the only light source cast distorted moving shadows of varied sizes from all the different rock formations. Nick spoke up startling Jillian and James and said, "This is the creepiest room yet. How would we ever see or discern unwelcome shadows here with us? It's too dark and our lights cast shadows everywhere."

Jillian with a shaky voice nervously whispered, "This is a large tunnel and cave system, and it seems endless. I never expected to find all of this, and we could be in over our heads here. I am concerned we could easily become disoriented and lost in the darkness and vastness of these caves."

They decided to try going left first and placed markers near the tunnel so they could identify the way back. James also wrote down identifying rock formations in the area. Nick pointed out more tunnel offshoots leading away from the large cave area. James contacted the others to let them know about the massive cave discovery. Matt, Aden, and Angie were still in a tunnel as were Bella and Chris.

James, Jillian, and Nick were exploring the expansive cave as they walked. They could see growing shadows with the light creating optical illusions. Jillian heard rustling in the high ceiling areas and moved her flashlight around to see the quick-moving shadows on the ceiling. Jittery and on edge as if waiting for something to happen, she stopped walking and jumped as she was startled by the moving shadows in her peripheral vision. James was also checking it out and yelled "bats! They are bats!" Jillian sighed and started walking again. They were all feeling anxious and jumpy.

It was at that moment that Jillian saw a human-like shadow to her left walking along the wall. She flashed her light in that direction and the figure disappeared. A cold chill went down her back as she shivered. She whispered, "I just saw a shadow that looked human over there!" Nick and James looked over and quietly waited. Minutes later they all saw the human-like figure walking close to the wall behind them. As they watched, the shadow became more visible and began to look familiar. James softly said, "I believe that is Flannery Token." They continued to watch as the shadow figure became identifiable as a human figure, and the clothes were detailed enough to be recognizable. Jillian verified it looked very much like the man they saw in the museum and in the photos on the bulletin board in the diner. Nick said, "He does not seem threatening." Jillian said under her breath, "I wonder why he is here?"

They stood very still and watched this figure that was now standing in front of the wall facing them. Although he had not been a threatening entity towards them so far, seeing him in the dark cave environment following other more threatening experiences made them act carefully and cautiously. As they stood and watched his image, the image of Flannery Token began to fade away. Jillian found herself calling out to him and said, "Wait! Please wait!" The image disappeared as quickly as it had materialized. She said, "Let's wait a few minutes to see if he returns. He must be showing himself for a reason."

After some time went by, Nick suggested they take a water break and found a low rock formation where they could sit. Jillian turned on the voice recorder to see if they could communicate with Flannery Token. They sat quietly and carefully listened. Jillian spoke loudly and asked, "Is this the spirit of Flannery Token? If so, why are you here? Can you help us?" They waited a few more minutes and Nick re-wound the tape. They waited patiently listening to recorded silence until they heard a voice. The spirit answered, "In the books, you will find the key." It was a very soft, muffled voice that was barely discernible. Following the spoken sentence there was silence on the recording. Jillian quickly rewound the tape to listen again. "In the books, you will find the key", the voice said. Jillian quickly hit record and asked, "Is this Flannery Token? Are you trying to help us?" They waited and then played back the tape. A voice softly said. "Yes." Then they heard a loud, screechy scream so ominous it forced them to cover their ears and scramble to turn down the volume. The scream lasted about five seconds and then the tape went silent again. Jillian turned off the tape with a click that echoed throughout the cave. Nick felt shaky and with a wavering, soft voice said, "What was that?" James shook his head and said, "I believe Flannery Token is trying to help us, but he is not alone." "Something else wanted to be heard. Jillian shivered and James shifted uncomfortably as he pointed his flashlight around where they were sitting. They were in the dark, in a large cave with no physical tools to defend themselves with. They could be surrounded by those creatures, and by other spirits and would not even know it. Nick thoughtfully said, "What books do you think he was speaking of?" Jillian answered, "The only books we have found so far are the books about spells and curses." She took the books out of her bag again, and they bent over with flashlights to look more closely. She opened the spell book and went through the pages. The book was heavily bound with a thick brown and black cover and was stiff as she opened it. She flipped through the pages noticing nothing new and turned to the last page. At the end of the book, she noticed a darker-colored section on the inside back cover. Running her fingers across this dark area she was able to peel back the protective paper to reveal a small space that was carved out. They gasped as she pulled out a small antique-looking key. James wondered out loud, "What do you think is in that drawer?"

Coming to the same conclusion they all wondered if this key opened that drawer. "We have to try it!" Jillian exclaimed. Nick suggested they backtrack to that large room with the table and pulpit to see if the key opened the drawer. Excitedly James and Jillian agreed.

James walked over to the tunnel with the markings and picked them up. "This is the way!"

Chapter 14

Revelations

Matt, Aden, and Angie continued through the tunnel. It was dark, and the slightest noise created echoes. The noise from walking was loud in the narrow space. Matt led the way with Angie in the middle and Aden following behind. Angie noticed how quiet it was behind her. The sound of Aden's feet scuffing the floor as he walked was now silent. She turned around to find no one behind her. She shouted, "Matt stop! Aden is not behind me, and I can't see him down the tunnel." They both turned around and quickly walked the other direction. They found him sitting on the ground, leaning against the tunnel wall with his head down. Matt asked, "Aden, what is going on? We almost lost you." Aden looked up and shrugged his shoulders. "I am feeling very tired and need to stop and rest for a while." Angie looked at Matt and they exchanged concerned glances. Aden did not sound like himself, and something was off. Matt encouraged him to get on his feet and suggested maybe they needed to get him out of the space. Both Matt and Angie understood the risk Aden took when he entered the tunnels. They recognized the signs he might be in trouble. Matt communicated with the others and told them they needed to walk Aden out of the tunnels and the three started walking back.

Matt picked up the markers as they backtracked through the tunnels. They walked quickly, preoccupied with the possibility of encountering the shadow figures that chased them out before. They walked for what seemed like almost too long. Matt said, "Haven't we gone too far? We should be reaching the staircase to the attic by now." Angie agreed it seemed too far and she began to wonder if they were lost. Aden walked slowly and in silence. Angie flashed her light toward his face and screamed. His face looked aged, shrunken, and wrinkled, with big bulbous eyes. His eyes were very red with sloshing liquid inside. He was hunched over, with long skinny arms and legs. His clothes were hanging on his thinner frame. His fingers were bony and thin with yellowed nails. His hair was now hanging in long white wisps. He smiled at her and exposed long sharp yellow teeth. She screamed again and Matt flashed his light that way. He jumped back when he looked at Aden's face. His flashlight dropped and Angie's flashlight went out. They had stopped and were standing next to Aden, who had become something else… in the dark.

Angie grabbed Matt's arm and they backed away from where Aden was standing. Trembling, Angie started to shake her flashlight hoping to get it working again. Matt moved his feet around on the floor searching for the flashlight he dropped. He heard Aden breathing long, loud, raspy breaths nearby. The search for the flashlight became more desperate. Angie's light turned on again and she flashed it on the ground. Matt spotted the flashlight and grabbed it. They both used the lights to find Aden. Angie's light shook as she trembled. Aden was not with them anymore. They searched the tunnel in both directions and could not find him. Angie asked, "Where did he go?" Matt used the walkie to explain what happened to the group. They were all very panicked and agreed to retreat back to the staircase. Matt and Angie hoped to be able to find the way back. Matt marked the area where they were standing when Aden disappeared. James, Jillian, and Nick were going back to the room with the drawer to try using the key, and then they would return.

Angie led the way with Matt following close behind. After a few minutes, he thought he heard something behind him. Glancing back, he noticed a shadow moving. He told Angie, "Move quickly, something is following us!" She started to run and as they did, Matt glanced behind him again to see more shadows following them. The shadows were moving on the sides and the ceiling of the tunnel, and they were gaining speed. They came to another area with tunnel offshoots and Angie ran down the closest one with Matt following. Matt looked behind him and the shadows were no longer following them. He told Angie she could slow down. Out of breath, they stopped for a moment. Matt heard voices close by. It was Chris and Bella. He spoke loudly and asked for Chris. Chris answered and Matt and Angie followed the sound of the voices. They walked out of the tunnel and into the room with the staircase to find Chris and Bella waiting for them.

James, Jillian, and Nick arrived in the room with the table and the pulpit. Jillian immediately rushed to the table and felt underneath. She found the drawer and knelt on the floor. Using her flashlight, she shined the light on the drawer and the keyhole. Using the old key, she tried to fit it in the keyhole. It was a tight fit and when it was inserted, she turned the key with force. Dust floated everywhere and she coughed while opening the drawer. It was not possible to look inside the drawer, as it was located so tightly underneath the table, so she used her fingers to pull out what she found. An intricate wooden box. She placed the wooden box on the table, and they crowded around it. They took turns holding and examining the box, fascinated. Jillian spoke up, "Flannery Token wanted us to find this box. We need to open it." Nick whispered, "Maybe we need to open it when we are with the others." They looked at one another and knew they had to open the box immediately. James used the walkie to inform the group about what they found, and the plan to open the box. The box had a latch, and it was easy to move. They held their breaths while Jillian opened the lid.

The flashlights were quickly pointed toward the contents inside the box. Immediately they recognized what was inside. It was an amulet like the one discovered during the Edin house investigation. She took it out and examined it. The memory of the amulet discovery was still fresh in their minds.
It was another shiny amulet with an old leather chain. The memory of the first discovery came flooding back.

Jillian carefully picked the amulet up out of the box, and they all inspected it. It had some sort of precious stone placed inside an ornate silver setting. It was quite large. Jillian noticed a piece of the amulet was missing like the amulet they found at the Edin house investigation. She looked carefully inside the box and found the compartment underneath. She lifted this compartment and found the missing piece. They all retained vivid memories of what happened after finding the amulet during the Edin house investigation. Jillian had taken the broken piece and placed it in the empty space fitting it in like a puzzle. The piece melted into the amulet seamlessly and the amulet was complete. Jillian remembered before, as she held it when she thought she noticed a light or reflection growing brighter inside the middle of the stone. She had asked everyone to turn off their flashlights for a moment. They stood in complete darkness and could see a bright blue light shining from the amulet. They all gazed at this light in amazement. There was no explanation for why this amulet could be powering a light inside. They stood for what seemed like a long time staring at this light and Jillian realized this might be dangerous. They were all too mesmerized by this light. Jillian broke the piece off the amulet. She quickly placed the pieces back into the box keeping them separated as they were found. They all snapped out of the daze they were in and recognized the power and danger this amulet could bring. They would need to be careful. The amulet found during the Edin house investigation was essential. The power of the amulet was shown to them when the team fought for their lives and souls. It saved them and created danger and risk they could not have ever anticipated.

Possessing and using the amulet was a double-edged sword. With its use and the power that comes with it they learned very quickly it is a blessing and a curse. This memory was truly clear, and they understood the potential power of this second amulet.

Jillian thought about the history and stated, "Susanna was the mother to me, and Mary was the mother to James. Susanna and Mary had married into the Edin family so many years ago. Susanna had written about an amulet. A possession that belonged to William Luster many years before. The first amulet was destroyed when Susanna and Mary performed the original banishment spell. That dark night when both Susanna and Mary perished, and we were so young. That night when James and I were practically babies and so innocently entered through the portal that was created by the power of the dark magic. It all still seems so impossible, but we know it to be true. During the Edin house investigation, we found the second amulet. Now we have a third. These amulets could be powerful and misused if in the wrong hands. Chris keeps the second amulet safe and under lock and key at the estate. So now there is a third and we will need to protect it."

They hurriedly packed up the gear and Jillian, James and Nick started back in the direction of the staircase room. The others were waiting for them and there was great urgency to start the search to find Aden. As they walked quickly through the tunnels Jillian, James, and Nick listened and looked for any signs of Aden along the way. It was a quiet walk with the three trying to process this latest information. James carried the backpack on his shoulder, protecting it with one hand. He could feel the box containing the amulet moving slightly within the backpack with each step he took. It was reassuring to feel that movement and holding the backpack with one hand felt like an extra step of protection. It was valuable, powerful, and dangerous cargo. He took a long breath as he walked. Jillian noticed James seemed deep in thought. She reached out her hand and placed it on his shoulder. With his other hand, James touched hers and they continued through the tunnel. After about thirty minutes they entered the staircase room to find Bella, Chris, Matt, and Angie discussing how to find Aden. There were numerous challenges due to the labyrinth of tunnels and caves.

They stopped talking when Jillian, James, and Nick arrived. Matt and Chris wanted to see the amulet. They all stood in a circle as Jillian removed it from the backpack and opened the box to reveal it. They looked on in amazement. They wondered what it could mean. Did this amulet have the same power? There was instantly a lot of excited chatter. Chris took a step back and paused for a moment. The others turned to look at him. He whispered, "I need to show you all something." Bending over he opened his backpack and took out an object and placed it on the table. They all pointed light at the object and gasped. It was the box that held the second amulet. He opened it to show them. He said, "I brought this to use if we got in trouble and needed it." So now they had two amulets. Jillian asked, "I wonder if they were created to work together? Or should they be kept apart?" Bella said, "I wish they came with instructions. It might be dangerous to have them together even in the same room. These two amulets have not been together for many years. How could we know what might happen?"

Jillian looked at James and he knew what she was thinking. He offered to hold the amulets together to see what information he could absorb from them. He took both amulet pieces out of the boxes and held one in each hand. He sat on the floor against the wall while they all kept flashlights on to illuminate the room as much as possible. Angie gasped as she noticed the amulets changed color while he was holding them. They were missing the second pieces yet were still glowing bright bluc. The wind picked up and the energy became explosive as James started absorbing information. The team stood their ground as the hurricane-like winds continued to sweep around them. The noise was overwhelming. Jillian watched James carefully to make sure he was ok. He was focusing with his eyes closed and remained calm with the chaos surrounding him. After a few minutes, the winds slowed down and the energy in the room became calm. The amulets stopped glowing. When it was still in the room again, James opened his hands and Chris took the amulets and placed them back in the boxes. James was sweating and looked exhausted.

They waited in the dark staircase room with only the light of the flashlights. James opened his eyes and asked for time to get his thoughts together. He needed to sort out the information he received.

After some time passed James whispered, "These amulets are ancient. They were created centuries ago by a secret society located in a monastery run by monks, and religious leaders of that time who were part of the original organization tasked with finding Integrals. The original 'Nature's Integral

Spirit'. They had been involved for centuries in uncovering and fighting evil. People just like us, who risked their lives to save humanity without humanity ever knowing they existed. However, they were eventually discovered, and the villagers did not understand. The villagers assumed that the monks and others working out of this monastery – those who were part of this secret society, were all evil and practicing dark arts for nefarious purposes. The villagers blamed this organization for all the misfortunes plagued by the village. This took place in the dark ages when day-to-day life was challenging and misfortune, struggle and hard times were a normal part of life. The members of this secret society located in this monastery found out they had been discovered. They sent members to the far ends of the globe, handing off these responsibilities to noble, wealthy families to continue the secret practices privately to prevent being discovered. Great lengths were taken to protect these secrets. The important responsibilities and mission would remain within the same family lines forever, as they continue to exist today. These families are responsible for finding the integrals of their generation, helping them to learn to use what powers they possess, and helping to fight evil to protect our world as we know it. Like Chris and Bella and their family."

James continued; "The remaining members of the monastery were brutally killed by the villagers who did not understand the practices that appeared like dark magic. The members of this monastery were forever blamed by the villagers for all the darkness and hardships of the time, not realizing that this secret society had been working to protect them. It was a tragedy the remaining living members of the monastery could never allow to happen again."

James paused and said, "Three amulets were originally created. They were sent to three of these noble families located far apart from one another. These amulets were never supposed to be used together. The power would be too strong for anyone to manage. They were created to assist in the fight against evil by giving a way to open the portals or doors when needed, and to close them. If the amulets are used together, they will conjure too much energy and could attract spirits from all over the other realms and dimensions. They could open more than one portal or door at once. The dark spirits would be attracted to the energy, and it could create a gathering so powerful it might not be containable."

James took a long breath looked at the team members, and continued, "William Luster was born with extraordinary gifts as an integral. He attracted an ancient evil when practicing dark magic. He lived in Susurrous Pines, a place where there had been great pain and suffering and violent death over many years. These negative energies attracted evil. This town became a beacon for evil. Some spirits have the power to break through the portal and move in and out of our world for brief periods of time. They are seeking the ability to break through to our world and stay here. They have been slowly acquiring power over numerous years. These ancient evil forces have been gaining strength for centuries, waiting for an opportunity. They have been gaining followers and momentum over this time. I am afraid the amulets if used together could give them everything they need to fully create the scourge."

Jillian asked, "What about the good spirits like Flannery Token? What will happen to the good spirits who are stuck in transition?" Bella said, "If we believe there is a better place like a heaven where spirits can go, we should be able to help the benevolent spirits crossover if they are ready." "They are here for a reason. Perhaps they have unfinished business. Maybe helping us will allow spirits like Flannery Token to move on."

Chris looked at Jillian, James, and the team with a worried look and said, "There is more." The team waited silently for him to finish. He continued, "Ancient evil does exist as we are learning through our experiences and research. There are other ways these spirits can enter our world. I learned of a process called soul switching or soul merging. It describes a process where a person's soul can be temporarily extracted and replaced by something else, or a soul could be subdued into submission and basically imprisoned within the body allowing something else to take over. I read about this in our ancestral books. This can happen even before a child is born. It has never been officially documented but the possibility is written in the ancient documents and the ancestral books. This event or process would be extremely difficult to detect. The original human soul can be merged with the ancient evil. This being would have extraordinary power. This being would have an intense connection with the spirit world and might possess the ability to control it. I think about the grave and potentially catastrophic possibilities if a human soul who is also an integral with integral abilities was merged or fused with a dark spirit."

Angie asked, "Why have you waited to tell us about this soul switching or soul merging concept until now?" Chris said in a whisper, "I believe Aden could be one of these beings." The group gasped. Angie said in an upset and panicked voice, "Why do you think this?" Chris responded, "All of his reported experiences through childhood and in adulthood including our past investigation, as well as what has happened tonight." Angie said in tears, "What can we do?" She knew in her heart Chris might be correct about Aden. The being she saw in the tunnels was not Aden it was something else. She had pushed away the horrible image of Aden as that creature. It was too painful to think about. Now she closed her eyes and shuddered as she thought about that creature Aden had become. The detailed image of that creature was so fresh and clear in her mind. Chris answered, "I believe the Aden we know is still in there, but at times he is in a battle for his soul. He is fighting against the power of these spirits without fully developing and understanding his own abilities. I am hoping we can help him. We have pulled him out of this before." Angie remained quiet while hanging on to those hopeful words. She found herself silently and desperately bargaining for Aden's safe return although who or what she might be bargaining with she was did not know. Was she communicating with God? She was not a religious person and was at a loss about how to hold out hope for an external influence to help Aden. Then it dawned on her that maybe the secret weapon to protect Aden was his own inner strength within himself. This possibility provided additional reassurance to her.

James looked down at his hands that were previously holding both amulets. The group took a breath together as they realized the danger of possessing both. Chris said, "We need to keep the amulets in the boxes and keep them separated for now." "We can never let them get in the wrong hands."

"It could be the scourge that would be the end of days." James explained, "I saw fire, devastation, and desolation. I saw a world filled with the creatures we have seen. The human spirit taken over by an ancient evil. Everything we recognize that allows us to be human is gone. The remaining state of the world is unrecognizable."

They were all stunned by the latest information. The danger was unlike anything they had ever experienced. They stood together in the darkness of the staircase room feeling overwhelmed, exhausted and frightened. It was about 1:00 in the morning.

Angie spoke up and asked, "What are we going to do about Aden? He is still somewhere in the tunnels." They stood and thought for a moment. It was clear a rescue mission needed to happen. Matt said, "The tunnel and cave system down here is very extensive and complex. We need to find a way to search for him without getting lost. It should involve staying together this time now that we know the risks." They began to gather up the gear once again. Chris said very quietly, "I think we need to separate these two amulets. One needs to be placed safely somewhere far away from here." Bella nodded her head in agreement. She whispered, "We need to take one of the amulets back to the estate and place it in a safe." Chris agreed and the team decided Chris and Bella would immediately take the long drive back to the estate with the amulet while the remaining team would stay in the tunnels to search for Aden. Jillian would hold on to one amulet in case they needed it for protection.

Chris and Bella would meet them back at the Chateau sometime tomorrow. They said their goodbyes and Chris and Bella started the climb up the staircase to the attic.

Chapter 15

The Mystery of Evil

Bella and Chris reached the attic and from there walked quickly to the room where they gathered necessary belongings. Minutes later they were walking down the front steps to the car. Chris carefully placed the bag containing the amulet on the seat behind him. It was a very dark night with thick clouds blocking any chance of moonlight. The night was thick with dense fog. Bella spoke with a concerned voice, "It's very quiet, and there is so much fog we can barely see in front of us." Chris said, "We just need to get out of town and clear the mountain area and the rest of the drive should be trouble-free." He pulled out of his parking spot and started down the long driveway away from the Chateau.

As they drove down the driveway the fog grew thicker and denser. Chris was driving very slowly and struggled to see the road. Bella started to wonder if they would be able to drive out of the town safely. The driveway was surrounded on both sides by tall trees. The fog was drifting a bit with the wind and occasionally she could see through the window the outline of the trees as the car slowly drove by. Suddenly her eyes were diverted to a particular tree. A bank of thick fog was slowly drifting over this tree and its branches. There was movement on a branch and Bella thought she saw red eyes through the fog. It was a brief view and she let out a soft gasp as she told Chris, "I think I see something in the trees!" He looked at the line of trees and jumped in his seat when he too noticed movement on the tree limbs. Shadows were slithering across the tree trunks and long branches. As she continued to watch, the shadows became more visible, and she recognized the creatures and their familiar shapes and movement. They were crawling and creeping around on the tree trunks and branches. The fog briefly lifted with a wind gust, and they could see the gray-colored creatures with wrinkled skin and long white wisps of hair hanging from their heads. They had skeletal heads with sunken eye sockets, long, thin legs, and arms, and they crawled on all fours, hunched down low on the tree limbs. The long-yellowed nails dug deep into the tree branches causing chips and chunks of tree branches to rain down. Bella and Chris both screamed as they could see the red eyes glowing in the branches as the fog drifted around the trees.

Chris yelled, "I think they are following us!" He started to drive faster and as he did, the movement in the trees also grew faster, keeping up with the car's speed. The creatures were crawling quickly along the branches and jumping from tree to tree. Bella and Chris could hear loud raspy growling and high-pitched howling that sounded like screams. The noise was deafening. Sharp, pointed, yellow teeth could be seen when the creatures snarled and wailed. Bella screamed in a panic as the creatures were now also down on the ground moving around the car. Chris continued erratically driving as he tried to avoid all the creatures surrounding the car. He started hitting them one after one as they crawled and jumped on the road in front of the car. Bella and Chris could feel the car hitting large bumps in the road, as they ran over the creatures.

They turned on the main road with the fog growing so thick Chris had no visibility. He continued to drive believing he had no alternative. Bella was frantically looking all around them as the numbers of the creatures surrounding the car grew. She yelled in a panicked and terror-stricken voice, "There must be hundreds of them!" Chris was not sure what to do and continued with the plan to reach the covered bridge leading out of town. Bella screamed as one of the creatures landed on the hood of the car. Chris hit the breaks and it slid off and landed on the ground. Chris quickly hit the gas and ran over it. More creatures were jumping on the back and front of the car. Chris sped up as he thought he could see the covered bridge in front of them at a distance. As he sped up another creature jumped on the hood and this time, before Chris could abruptly stop, it smashed the windshield with its long arms. They both screamed as Chris tried to fight off the creature with one hand and drive with the other. Bella was fighting another one that had broken through the window next to her, and she was frantically trying to hit the thin gray arms with wrinkled sagging skin that were reaching through trying to grab her. The chaos in the car proved to be too much. Chris started to lose control, the car skidded, turned, and hit a tree with a loud bang. The night went silent. The creatures slowly crept away disappearing in the fog and the growling, wailing, and howling faded off into the distance.

Minutes later Chris began to stir. He slowly woke up and felt his head. He had a large knot on his forehead near the hairline. With his head aching, he opened his eyes and looked around. It was still very dark, and the car was smashed into a tree. He started to remember what happened and quickly glanced to his right to check on Bella. She appeared to be unconscious, and he moved toward her. She too had a large bump on the side of her forehead. He gently shook her. She made a moaning noise and he continued to gently shake her. He spoke loudly to get her attention, "Bella, wake up! You need to wake up! We have been in an accident." She slowly began to stir and immediately started rubbing her head. She whispered, "I have such a headache." Then she abruptly sat up, remembering what happened before the accident. She groaned and rubbed her arm on the window side. She looked at her hand and it was covered with blood. She looked at her arm and it had long, deep and bleeding claw marks all the way up and down her arm. Chris looked and said, "Oh my God, look at your arm!" Bella moaned again and said softly. "It actually is not that bad. Looks worse than it feels."

They both stayed in the car for a few minutes gathering themselves. Chris surveyed the landscape surrounding the car and did not see any movement and did not notice anything unusual. No movement in the trees, no red eyes, and no sign of those creatures. They disappeared as quickly as they had materialized. The creatures hit by the car were no longer on the road. The thick fog that had completely enveloped the car had dissipated. It was a clear, dark, quiet night again. They started to pry themselves out of the seats. The front end and the passenger rear side of the car were crushed. They must have spun around and somehow hit the tree twice Chris thought. They slowly extracted themselves from the car and were standing next to the tree. Then Chris remembered the bag he left in the back seat. The bag that contained the amulet. He walked back and forced the door open. He went to pick up the bag and realized the seat was empty. He quickly checked the floor in the back seat area, and the bag was not there. He checked the front seat area thoroughly in case the bag was projected into the front of the car during the impact. It was not there. Bella realized what was happening and said, "Maybe the bag was thrown outside of the car during the impact. The front windshield and side window are broken." They both checked around the car, and underneath. It was not there. They increased the perimeter around the car and checked farther away in case it had been thrown a distance. It was not anywhere around the car.

Bella then proclaimed in a very ominous tone, "Those creatures were after us because of the amulet. They wanted the amulet." Chris quietly whispered, "And they got it. We cannot let this happen. The dark spirits cannot use the amulet."

Chris got on the walkie and called James. He told James what happened and that they were heading back to the Chateau. Chris realized that all this time the dark spirits might have been listening to the conversations. Learning more about the amulets and their power. Understanding the power, they would obtain if in possession of the amulets. He told James it was not safe to speak over the walkie. Jillian, James, and the rest of the team were entering the tunnels to search for Aden. Chris and Bella would catch up with them after they quickly bandaged their wounds. James understood the importance of keeping the other amulet safe. They were in danger being down in the caves and tunnels with that amulet. He could only hope the dark spirits did not know they had it.

Bella and Chris started the walk back to the Chateau. It was a long walk, and they were feeling impatient. Walking fast they talked about the night events. Chris whispered, "Those creatures were organized and seemed to be working together. They were trying to kill us to get what they needed. They might think they did kill us." Bella spoke softly and said, "I am thinking about that experience. It was terrifying and I knew we were fighting for our lives. At the same time, I also felt a connection with those creatures. I could sense what they were feeling. It was desperation, hopelessness, extreme anger and hostility, futility, and agony. The worst kinds of emotions. Emotions that would allow for the worst kind of atrocities. Kind of like what I think it would feel like to be in Hell." She went on to say, "If these dark spirits inhabited our world, humanity would be wiped out in a matter of days. They would stop at nothing." The urgency of the walking increased. Bella's arm was dripping blood from the deep claw marks. They needed to get back to the tunnels and caves to meet up with the others.

Chapter 16

The Search for Aden

In the tunnels, the team stayed close together. They focused on listening for sounds of movement. They searched with flashlights down the tunnels for any visible sign of Aden. They remained quiet this time, attempting not to give away the presence of the team. They walked and worried about where Aden was and what was happening to him. Jillian and James remembered well what happened during the Edin house investigation. They remembered how he lost time with no memory of what happened. How he looked when he went through the transformation of turning into something else. It had been scary and unnerving. Jillian liked Aden so much and was wracked with relentless concern after the Edin house investigation. When that investigation wrapped up, he never completely returned to his normal self. He continued to have difficulty sleeping and kept his windows taped shut and covered. It was as if he was trying to keep something out even though he lived on an upper floor. He always looked tired with heavy bags under his eyes. She wondered why he was interested in participating in the investigation of Susurrous Pines. She thought maybe with this investigation he might find answers.

James had the bag over his shoulder with one hand over it. He needed to keep it close. It was a terrible idea to have the bag down in the tunnels with them after Bella and Chris reported getting chased and attacked by the creatures. The level of intelligence guiding the dark spirits was high. They were working together for a combined purpose. James whispered to the team, “It seems as if the dark spirits and the guiding evil are trying to acquire all of the remaining amulets. They knew Bella and Chris had an amulet and they were trying to leave Susurrous Pines with it. The creatures stopped them and might have killed them in the process. What do we do with the bag now? Can we sneak it out of town? They cannot acquire the contents of this bag." Nick spoke up and very quietly said, "We cannot talk about this now. We are already down here and need to find Aden. Let's focus on that for now."

They moved forward in silence and fear. They were plodding through the tunnel that had many offshoots. As they walked by each new tunnel entrance, they pointed flashlights as far down the tunnel as possible. Matt stopped short as he walked by one tunnel offshoot and used his light. He softly said, "I just saw movement down this tunnel!" They all walked to the entrance using the lights. There was a tall shadow clearly visible moving slowly through the tunnel and walking away from them in a slow sauntering gait. Nick went first, next was Matt, Jillian, Angie, and last James. They ran carefully and quietly through the dark tunnel trying to catch up with the shadow. As they approached it was clearly Aden wearing recognizable clothes. They ran faster, and it seemed like they should be catching up with him. He was always slightly out of reach in the distance in the dark. Finally, they turned a corner, and he was there facing a wall. Angie spoke to him and whispered, "Aden, we are here. Are you all right? We need to leave the tunnels now." There was silence. She placed her hand on his shoulder and he slowly turned toward her. His face had returned to normal although his expression was blank. He did not appear to recognize her at all. She guided him toward them and in the direction out. They had a long walk out of the tunnels, and he willingly walked with them.

Every team member tried to get him to speak without success. Jillian whispered, "This reminds me of before. He would not answer us or interact for a period of time and did not remember anything about this happening after." They walked as quickly as they could while guiding him out. They turned back into the main tunnel and kept going. Finally reaching the staircase room, they guided Aden up the stairs. When all the team members were back in the attic room, Bella and Chris walked in. Bella had bandages on a large part of her arm and her forehead. Chris had bandages on his head and on his ankle. They looked like they had been through a lot. Bella sighed out of relief when she saw Aden although she recognized he was not in a good place. The blank stare looked familiar. Angie said, "Let's get Aden back to his room so he can try to sleep it off. Someone will need to stay with him. We should take shifts." They all agreed and walked back to the rooms. It was almost dawn and it had been an incredibly long night. They were exhausted and needed to sleep. Matt offered to take the first shift with Aden. They all agreed to keep the walkies on just in case Matt needed help.

Jillian and James opened the door to the room and Mags happily greeted them. She was awake and ready to play and seemed sad that they were in bed sleeping within minutes. Mags jumped on the bed and settled in between them with a loud dog sigh and closed her eyes.

Chapter 17

The Mysterious Ally

The Chateau fell silent as the team slept. The sun rose over the town on a clear cold day. Jillian woke up to the sound of Mags snoring loudly. She sat up and noticed how bright the room was. The sun was out and shining brilliantly through the windows. She checked the clock to see it was 1 pm. She glanced over at James who was still sleeping soundly. He was holding the bag tightly while he slept. She carefully slipped the bag out of his grip to make sure the amulet was still inside. She opened the bag and could see the wooden box. Breathing a sigh of relief, she placed the bag back in his hands and he instinctively tightened his grip. She thought to herself, "The dark spirits must not know we have this amulet. They would be aggressively seeking it if they knew." She decided to get dressed and see if anyone else was awake yet. After dressing she walked toward the door. This got the attention of Mags who was ready to go outside. Jillian grabbed her leash, and they left the room. Today she decided to take Mags outside using the rear exit from the Chateau. She had not investigated the extensive backyard area and she felt compelled to look around. Maybe she could find another clue. It was a beautiful, bright day and she felt safe in the light for the moment.

She found no one on the first floor and assumed the team was still sleeping. She walked behind the main staircase and down a long hall to the back doors. Mags was energetic and happy to be going outside. She wagged her tail and did a little excited hop every few steps. Jillian opened the doors and entered an old garden area. There were benches, and areas that were once covered with beautiful and ornate gardens. Now it was unkempt and overgrown. There were decrepit old sculptures and statues throughout the garden area. At one time this must have been very nice, she thought. Mags happily checked out the old shrubs and sniffed around the garden beds. They followed an overgrown cobblestone path that seemed to extend quite far. As they walked the sky grew cloudy. The sun peeked in and out from the clouds. The wind picked up and blew through the tall pines nearby. She loved the sound of the wind whispering through the pines. Susurrous Pines is a perfect name for this town, she thought. The sound of the wind blowing through the plentiful tall, old pine, spruce, and fir trees in the area was a constant.

They continued walking and she could see buildings at the edge of the forest at a distance. It appeared to be a large, dilapidated barn and an additional outbuilding. The barn was quite large and as they approached, she decided to go inside. The big barn door swung open, and they stepped inside. The roof was falling apart, and the sun shined through the gaps creating interesting shadows along the walls and floor. There was a main aisle with barn stalls lining both sides. It was clear this barn had not been used in an exceedingly long time. It smelled musty and damp, and there was a smell of decaying wood. Dust and dirt flew into the air as they walked and disturbed the earth underfoot. The dust was visible in clouds floating around in the sun-filled areas. Jillian walked with Mags slowly past each stall imagining what this barn must have looked like when it was in operation. Horses in each stall with workers using pitchforks and carrying buckets. The sound of horses stomping feet and swishing tails.

They came to the end of the aisle, and she looked up to see the hayloft area. There was a long ladder leading up to the loft. The ladder looked like it might support her weight and she was curious about what might be up in the loft. Standing at the bottom of the ladder she tested the first stair. It felt solid enough, so she continued up. One step at a time with Mags standing at the bottom watching her. Slowly she climbed the ladder steps. She did come across a couple of steps that were soft when she stepped down, but they held. She neared the top and climbed the last step. She felt around the loft floor to see if it would hold her weight. The loft floor was built with thick planks of wood, and she slowly stepped on it. Standing in one place near the ladder Jillian looked around. It was an empty, dark loft. She started back down the ladder. Mags was standing at the bottom growling and walking back and forth. Jillian stepped all the way down the steep ladder, and finally down on the floor giving her a pat on the head. Mags jumped and Jillian realized something was wrong. Mags was sensing something and felt threatened. She was looking at the far end of the barn toward a dark stall. Jillian started to walk over. As she approached the stall, Mags stayed close behind her growling. Jillian nervously laughed and said, "Brave girl." Walking closer to the stall Jillian started to feel anxious and uncomfortable. She began to have doubts about whether she should have come out to these buildings by herself. No one knew where she was, and no one would hear her if she got into trouble. She did bring the walkie with her, and she had her cell phone, however, if the team was still sleeping, they might not hear the call.

The barn was much darker on this side, and she could not see into the stall. Mags continued to growl with her hackles up. Jillian slowly turned to peer into the dark stall and suddenly Mags and Jillian were startled by a cat that jumped out of the shadows, screeching, and howling as it ran away from them. Jillian screamed and Mags barked and started to run after the cat. Jillian yelled for Mags to stop, and she listened and came trotting back. Jillian's heart was racing as she held her chest. She started to laugh. After all they had been through, she was not expecting to find a scared cat. Mags looked up at her wagging her tail. She seemed proud she had done her job. They walked through the back exit of the barn and toward the other two outbuildings.

Two smaller buildings located side by side appeared to be in the same condition as the barn. She walked into the building on the left first. Instantly she knew this was where they stored the farm tools and equipment. A lot of old equipment was still stacked or hanging in the main room of this building. Rusted out tools like pitchforks, scythes, saws, axes, blades, tillers, trowels, and sickles. They were all hanging from the ceiling and swinging around from the breeze the door created when she opened it. They were banging together and making loud clanging noises. There was another section of this building dedicated to horse care. Rusted out buckets, old bits, what remained of leather bridles, and a couple of old saddles covered in dust, mold, and rot. The building smelled of rusted iron and metal, dust, and mold.

As she stood still taking it all in, she asked Mags to sit in the doorway. Jillian did not want her walking through this area in case the chains the tools were hanging from were not secure. The chains were all rusted out and probably fragile. Jillian heard a loud noise above the sound of the tools hitting one another. The noise came from the far end of the building. She moved toward that direction telling Mags to stay. She carefully walked between the swinging tools. She thought she could see a shadow on the far wall. Then she heard a voice. It said in low deep sounds, "They have two amulets and are seeking the third." Jillian looked toward where the voice was coming from and continued to see the shadow. The shadow moved and she jumped, hitting one of the tools next to her and sending it swinging into more tools as the clanging became very loud. The voice spoke again, "They have two amulets and are seeking the third." Jillian immediately had a sense this was Flannery Token. He was trying to help them. She said, "How do they have two amulets? I thought the first amulet was destroyed?" The voice said, "It was not destroyed. It traveled through the portal at the same time you did. It was retrieved and kept close." The voice continued, "I must leave now." Jillian frantically said, "Wait! Wait! I need to talk to you!" It was quiet and the shadow was gone.

She stood still for a moment, realizing what he had said. She backed out of the building quickly and ran with Mags back to the Chateau. They ran through the garden area, through the back doors and up the main stairs, and into the room. James was sitting up by now and she sat on the bed. Mags jumped on the bed to greet James. Jillian started to explain to James what happened in the tool building. When she finished, he looked stunned. He picked up the bag that held the third amulet. They both understood the importance of the bag and its contents.

Chris and Bella were relaxing on the bed talking. Even though she was exhausted Bella was having trouble relaxing enough to fall asleep. Chris fell asleep first as she looked at her phone, tried to read a bit, and eventually grew sleepy.

Chris was walking on a dirt mountain road lined with tall trees and surrounded by thick forest as the sun was setting behind him. He was walking up a steep hill and as he crested the hill, he could see an enormous old stone structure with giant wooden doors. It appeared like an ancient stone manor with barns and livestock fields edged with wooden fencing. The stone manor house had smoke billowing out of the large chimney. Chris walked up and knocked on the wooden doors. The sound echoed throughout the large house. He noticed a wooden sign that said, "Open the door and speak to the resident keeper." He opened the door and walked in to find an empty hall. There was a large desk area with a chair, and hallways leading to the right and to the left. He decided to walk to the left. The hall was dimly lit with candles burning in iron sconces on the walls. The floors were made of stone and the hallway was very drafty. He could smell melted candle wax, burning wood from a fireplace, and the mineral smell of dirt. He walked past large stone doors on the right and left sides of the hallway. At the end of the hall, he discovered another set of large stone double doors and he opened them. The doors closed and locked behind him. He was standing in a huge chapel area with a pedestal and table in the middle. He could see ornate statues and sculptures and carved wood features around the windows. The center of the room was surrounded by rows of long bench seats that looked like pews. He heard whispering and looked over to see a group of men wearing brown hooded robes. They seemed to be engaged in an important discussion. The whispering sounded concerned, and maybe panicked. They appeared to be hiding behind a large wooden sculpture.

Chris thought these were monks, and he must be in a monastery. People could be heard running through the hallways outside the room. The footsteps and shuffling in the hall were moving closer. Chris was about to try to speak with the monks when there was a loud bang on the doors. They stayed low and quiet as more banging took place. The banging grew louder, and it was clear the doors were going to be broken down. A few more loud bangs and the doors fell to the floor with a loud crash. Bursting in, the villagers holding torches grabbed the monks and tethered their hands with thick rope. The villagers dragged the monks down the stone hall, and out the front doors. They dragged them to the edge of the forest where there were looped ropes hanging from trees. Chris could feel the fear and panic from the villagers and the monks. Chris woke up from the dream immediately before the monks were going to be brutally killed. He was clearly shaken, and Bella woke up as he sat up in a sweat. He explained the dream and how real it seemed. They attributed the dream to the story from James about the monks, the secret society, and the creation of the amulets. Chris felt as though he had actually been there and experienced it.

James got on the walkie and called Matt first. He asked Matt how Aden was. Matt reported Aden was still sleeping but all had been quiet. Matt had fallen asleep after a couple of hours of watching Aden and was feeling a bit more rested. James believed they all needed to meet in their room. Matt agreed to try to wake Aden and James would contact Chris, Bella, Angie, and Nick.

Matt sat next to Aden and spoke to him. Aden stirred and slowly sat up. He looked very tired, with dark circles around his eyes. Matt asked him how he was feeling. Aden answered, "I feel hungover like I have been asleep for days, or like I went on a drinking binge." Matt asked, "Do you remember what happened last night?" Aden sat for a moment and said, "I remember being down in the tunnels with you and Angie. I remember walking with Angie in front of me." "I don't remember anything else after that." He looked concerned and staring down at the blanket on the bed said, "It's happening again." Matt answered, "Something happened to you last night. We lost you for a period of time after you wandered off." "You were not yourself." Aden looked up at Matt through the long strands of hair falling over his face. Matt said, "Don't worry. We will figure this out. For now, we need to meet everyone else. Jillian and James want to debrief." Matt asked, "Can you get ready to meet the group?" Aden slowly stood up and walked to the bathroom. Matt took that as a yes.

The group met with Jillian and James, and they talked about what happened to Jillian out in the tool building. Chris looked shocked and said, "Is it possible? Could there be three intact amulets?" James whispered, "We need to be very quiet as we speak about this. They could be listening and watching everything we do. Chris and Bella were ambushed as they tried to leave Susurrous Pines with the amulet. The dark spirits knew about that amulet." James lifted the bag he was holding close to show the group the bag was safe. Bella softly spoke, "This all makes sense to me. We were drawn here. What if they have been using an amulet to move in and out of portals this whole time? We did not know they had that much power and ability. Given how many spirits we encountered it makes sense now." Nick, who had been noticeably quiet spoke up, "What happens now that they have two amulets?"

Angie looked at Aden carefully. He seemed deep in thought. He looked up at her and whispered, "I think I remember what happened last night. I was touched by one of the dark spirits and it forced me to connect with them. I understand now." Angie asked, "What do you understand?" He answered, "The ancient dark spirits have been waiting for centuries to break out into our world to escape purgatory. They have been manipulating broken spirits who may have been good and well-intended at one time. The dark spirits were able to turn them into something else. They may have been stuck in-between worlds with unfinished business and the dark spirits forced them into purgatory. However, they got there, these spirits are desperate and will do anything to permanently escape. I felt the anger and the desperation. There are so many." He continued, "They need all three amulets to permanently escape this purgatory from the dimension where they exist. They have a leader or leaders who are guiding them and understand about the power of the amulets." Jillian asked, "So what can we do to prevent this from happening? How do we prevent them from getting to this last amulet?" Bella whispered, "I don't think we will prevent them from acquiring the third amulet given what we just experienced with these creatures. It was overwhelming, and they were too strong. Our only hope is they do not know where we have placed it, or they do not know we have it with us."

Chris said, "Jillian, show us those outbuildings you found. We may find more clues." They all walked downstairs, out the back doors, through the old gardens, and toward the outbuildings. Jillian said, "I did not investigate the other outbuilding behind the barn." They walked through the old barn, checked out the tool building, and then walked to a third building. As they entered through the old wooden door, Angie let out a gasp, "It's an old well! Why would they build a structure around an old well?"

They stood in front of an old stone well. Jillian looked around the interior of the structure. There was nothing else in the building except for the well. Memories from the Edin house investigation flooded her mind. The old well behind the cabin, the dreams she had about the well, and the creatures trying to escape by climbing out. The team all seemed to be experiencing the same memories. Chris said, "This well looks very similar to the one we found before." Jillian slowly approached the well and looked over. It was very dark, and the bottom was not visible. She went outside picked up a few rocks and walked back in. She stood holding a rock over the well. "Let's see how deep this well goes." Jillian dropped the rock and they all waited. They waited for the sound of a thud from the rock hitting the ground at the bottom, or the sound of a splash from the rock landing in the water far below. They continued to wait. They all instinctively leaned farther over the top edge of the well waiting for the sound of the rock landing somewhere. The sound never happened, and they stood in silence. Bella asked, "What does that mean? Is the well so deep we could not hear the rock landing? Is it possible the well could be that deep? Wouldn't we have heard even a slight noise or echo of the rock landing even if the well is extremely deep?" No one had answers at this point. Jillian held another, larger rock over the well and let go. Again, they all waited and again they did not hear any sound of the rock landing. She tried one more time, holding a very large rock over the well. She held her breath and let go and they waited barely breathing as they tried to stay quiet. They all screamed and jumped away from the edge of the well as several bats moved quickly past them with fast flapping wings, flying indiscriminately out of the well. Everyone was breathing hard with Bella clutching her chest. Angie, in a breathless voice, said, "Oh my God I almost peed in my pants that scared me so much." There was a pause and they all laughed, including Angie. The laughter helped to temporarily interrupt the intensity of the situation. James said, "Thank you, Angie, I really needed that laugh." They all collected themselves and Chris noted, "Well, we did not hear the largest rock hit bottom, so I think we need to assume this well goes very deep."

They stood for a few more moments before Nick said, "Maybe we should go back inside and plan our next steps in the investigation". A loud noise startled them, and they all froze. A low grumbling, growling noise was growing louder and sounded as if it was coming from deep within the well. Aden said, "I think you awakened something when you dropped those rocks. They know we are here." The growling became screeching and then went back and forth between growling and screeching. The noise was getting louder, and they could hear movement in the well. Scraping, shuffling, and scuffing noises came from deep inside the well. Bella asked in a shaky voice, "Is something coming up out of the well?" The sounds of growling, snarling, screeching, scraping, and scuffing grew louder and closer. The panic set and the team instinctively backed up a few steps. Chris yelled, “We need to get out of here!” Instantly they all turned and ran out of the building. As they ran toward the Chateau, Jillian turned around to see if anything was following them. She did not see anything escaping from the building. Nothing yet. James is carrying the amulet in his bag and holding it close to his body. They all ran inside and shut the doors tightly. Angie said in a breathy voice, “Closing and locking the door makes me feel better but honestly will not make a difference. We all know they have many access points to this house and all around us.”

Breathing hard they stopped at the main entrance to regroup. Aden held his head low, looking at the floor with his long hair falling in front of his face. In a somber voice, he said, “They know we have the amulet.” The team looked at Aden, and then one another. The Chateau was quiet for now. They were exhausted and depleted and needed to rest and eat before taking on another long investigation night. Goals needed to be reset. They needed to find a way to obtain the other two amulets. The team decided to retreat to rooms for a little while before getting dinner.

Chapter 18

Mysterious Illusions

Jillian and James fell asleep as soon as their heads hit the pillows. They were so tired the danger of the situation was not enough to keep them from sleeping. After some time passed, Jillian opened her eyes and noticed Mags standing on the bed growling and staring at the door. Jillian sat up and observed a shadow moving around in front of the door in the hallway. A large, moving shadow was visible under the door. Mags was intently watching this shadow moving back and forth. Her eyes were focused on the space under the door and her head movements followed the shadow as it shifted and moved. They could hear shuffling and scraping noises coming from the hallway. Mags moved her ears in response to the sounds she heard. She continued to growl with the hackles on her back standing up.

Jillian glanced at James who was sleeping and holding the bag close while snoring. She walked toward the door and slowly opened it, expecting to see someone standing on the other side. There was no one there. She looked up and down the empty hallway. She heard a noise to her right and decided to walk down the hall. Mags went with her cautiously, sticking close by her side. They walked slowly down the poorly lit hall step by step. She noticed the musty, damp smell of the hallway. She looked down at her feet as she took each step. She could see the light puffs of dust kick up into the air as she walked. As they rounded the corner Jillian jumps back as she sees the woman with the long dark hair walking toward the top of the staircase. She called out to the woman and as she did Mags let out a loud growl. The woman turned to look at Jillian. Her hair began to change, turning from jet black to white. The woman was wearing the red dress. The dress was fitted in the bodice with a full-length skirt. It looked like a formal gown. The image of the woman wearing the bright colored red formal dress began to change. Within moments the dress was now hanging in gray tatters and strips as the woman's physical shape became shrunken and skeletal. No longer standing upright the woman was hunched over with a rounded back. Her skeletal spine could be seen clearly through the tattered dress. Her neck was bent up and she was looking up at Jillian. The woman's eyes were deep-set and now appeared to be sinking into her face. Her skin was gray and thin. Jillian watched in horror as this woman transformed in front of her into something else. The skeletal woman turned toward the stairs and slowly walked down as her long white and wispy hair blew around in a mysterious wind. As she walked down the stairs her image slowly disappeared until she was no longer visible. Mags continued to growl even after the woman was gone.

Jillian stood shaking, recognizing this must be the woman who was related to the Lusters. This woman who lost her life and her family in the mining accident. Now she was stuck here still feeling connected to the area. Maybe she had been changed into something else by the dark spirits. Maybe she was trying to hold on to what was left of her humanity. Jillian shuddered, thinking about what it must be like for some of the spirits stuck in that realm of purgatory. It was a version of hell. Not exactly what she had always thought of as hell, it was worse.

Jillian had these thoughts as she was standing at the top of the stairs trying to process what just happened. She felt compelled to look down at the stairs where the woman just walked. Mags was sniffing something on the stairs. Jillian let out a soft cry when she saw what Mags was sniffing. She said, "No!" She stepped back in absolute terror, immediately noticing her heart pounding in her chest. She placed her hand on her chest as if to symbolically support her heart. Jillian was looking at Russ on the stairs. Russ, a dark symbol from her childhood with a long history offering terrible memories for Jillian. He should have been locked away where she placed him and yet here, he sat, resting on the stair. She was sure it was another warning. The dark spirits know what they are afraid of. For Jillian, the fear of Russ went very deep and had been festering since she was a child. She held her breath, bent down, and scooped him up grimacing as she said to herself, "No, No, this cannot be happening."

In a panic, she turned and ran down the hall and back to the room to check on James. Mags was running along beside her with high energy, picking up on the fear and anxiety from Jillian. She burst into the room and woke James with the noise. Mags jumped on the bed. Jillian immediately noticed the bag with the amulet was gone. Yelling in a hysterical voice She said, "James where is the bag with the amulet?" He looked down, looked under the blankets, and jumped out of bed. He checked underneath the bed and all around, pulling the bedding off the bed. The bag was not there. They both checked all around the room, but it was gone. The amulet was gone. Jillian knew at that moment she had been tricked. The woman in the hall was a distraction so the bag and the amulet could be easily taken. She should never have left the room. She also harbored another suspicion. Aden had a connection with the dark spirits. Maybe they were listening through him. Maybe the dark spirits knew all about the amulet they were hiding after listening to their discussion and were planning to take it. Somehow, they knew where the amulet was, whether through Aden or by another way. She kept these thoughts to herself for now. They quickly mobilized the team to meet in the dining room.

Bella brought snacks from the car since this latest development would not give them time to eat a meal. She spilled the packaged food onto the table. They sat at the large, long dining room table on the first floor of the Chateau. The dining room was an exceptionally large space. Another aged and dilapidated room that must have been spectacular at one time. Now the wallpaper was faded, dusty, and peeling away in long strips. The window drapes were dingy and threadbare. What was left of the detailing in the fabric of the drapes once intricate and lavish was now hanging across the windows faded, and color bleached from years of sun exposure. The long table was dusty and surrounded by tall chairs. The chair seats were covered with worn and stained fabric that previously was a dark red color. The candelabra above the table held candles that had been used many times with the solidified drips along the sides. A dark and drab room rarely used these days. The long table allowed them to spread out and attempt to get comfortable while they discussed the next steps.

Chris spoke first, "We need to act quickly. I'm afraid we do not have much time now. The dark spirits have all three amulets now. If this power is unleashed, we could be at ground zero of the scourge." Jillian took out the books she had been carrying around. She placed the three books; Incantations in Darkness, Curses Book One, and Spells book two on the table. They passed around the books and Jillian said, "These books may give us ideas about what we can do. How we might be able to conjure up enough power and energy to fight this and get the amulets back." She went on to say, "We believe William Luster used dark magic and his gifts as an integral to increase his power and gain access to this other dimension. He accessed the power of evil for his own purposes. He may have cursed the town and even traded his soul for success. We may never know the whole story. For now, we need to assume he has an unlimited army of recruits to help him infiltrate our world. So maybe we can use his own tactics and practices against him. We have the power of at least two integrals in this room and possibly more. We need to search these books and use one of the spells, curses, or incantations." Bella with an excited voice asked, "Maybe we can find a spell that could temporarily neutralize the power of the amulets so we can intervene in the process while the portals are open?" Chris responded, "We all need to understand it might be impossible for us to survive this." Angie responded, "Maybe we are alright with that risk given the alternative of trying to survive the scourge which may also be impossible." James added, "Maybe we don't want to survive the scourge if it means turning into one of those creatures and forgetting our humanity. We need to prevent the scourge from happening in the first place."

They poured over the books, discussing the different spells and incantations, as well as the notes written in the margins of each book from William Luster's experiments. The notes offered insight into the results of his practices. James stopped on a page in the spell book. He asked, "What if we can find a spell that will reverse the energy from the amulets? When the dark spirits open the portal with the amulets, we could reverse the energy and send them back instead. Look at this!" He showed the team the spell he discovered. It was called the turnaround spell. Matt read out loud, "The turnaround or reversal spell turns the energy against the person trying to release it. It creates a backfire process." Angie said, "Can we find the elements called for in this spell? It requires feathers, a special kind of red clay or dirt, crystals, special candles, wind, and many other items." Jillian quickly responded, "I know where we can find feathers! Do you all remember the taxidermy birds we found in the basement? I also noticed reddish-looking soil in the outside garden." Nick said, "There is a large supply room next to the kitchen. There must be candles in that room somewhere." Matt responded, "We can do this. Let's split up and gather the elements. We can reconvene here in thirty minutes. We will do our best to complete the list of elements. That is the most we can do in such a brief period of time." They quickly wrote down the list of elements needed and scrambled out of the room.

They reconvened in the dining room thirty minutes later placing the gathered elements on the long table. Chris brought a large sports bag to place the elements in making it easier to carry in a rush. Jillian said, "I believe that main portal access point will be the well out back. We should set up our temporary altar to create the reversal spell in that building that surrounds the well. We need to light a fire and we can grab one of the large metal pots in the garden to contain the fire in the building." The group helped Chris place all of the elements in the sports bag. They walked with purpose through the Chateau and out the back door. Aden grabbed a large iron pot with a handle from the garden as they walked through.

There was an instant chill in the garden as they walked through. The air felt dense, and the sky grew cloudy. As they approached the well building the energy changed, and day turned into night. Jillian, James, Chris, Bella, Angie, Aden, Matt, and Nick all hesitated in front of the large wooden door. The weather turned stormy, and the feeling was noticeably ominous. The winds picked up and became very gusty. The wind grew so powerful it was difficult to stand. They were looking down, protecting their eyes from debris the wind was blowing around. The team jumped at the sound of loud thunder. Angie gasped at the sight of lightning flashing at close range. Aden said, "The dark spirits must be very close to opening the portal now." Jillian took a breath and opened the large wooden door. They quickly entered the well building and noticed the wind was inside the building as well. The noise from the wind was so loud they could barely be heard without yelling. Jillian knelt on the floor placing her bag down. The wind was whipping her hair around and she squinted her eyes to protect them from the searing air. The team worked with her to set up the large pot, the small altar, and all of the elements needed for the spell and the ritual. They needed to lean over the items to prevent them from blowing around. As they were arranging the items and setting up the fire in the pot, they felt the first tremor. Thunder, lightning, wind, and then the feeling of the earth shaking beneath them. Instinctively they all lowered themselves close to the floor as the ground shook violently.

James yelled through the loud din, "The portal must be open now!" The team collectively looked toward the well. Fog was wafting up and out of the well in gauzy, gray clouds. When the fog emerged out of the well it was immediately lifted away and scattered by the wind. There was a new urgency to get the spell started. Jillian took out the book and lined up the different elements while trying to read the instructions. The book pages were blowing, and Bella sat down next to her on the floor to hold the pages open. They set up protected areas that blocked the wind to keep the candles lit. Flashlights were set up to allow

Angie and Bella to see well enough. Angie looked over at Aden who appeared to be mesmerized by the display of energy being produced. Chris, Matt, and Nick were staring at the well opening and listening. Above the din of the wind, and the thunder, the low sounds of growling, and snarling could be heard. Matt, Chris, Nick, Aden, and Angie backed up to surround Jillian and Bella as they worked to get the spell started. The fire was set in the large pot, and they kept it going by keeping the fire low to prevent the strong wind from blowing it out. Jillian used a ceramic container placing the additional element ingredients inside before placing the container inside the large pot amid the fire. It became increasingly difficult for Matt, Chris, Nick, Aden, and Angie to hold positions facing outward in the circle surrounding Jillian and Bella. The wind was so strong they were being taken off their feet and losing balance. Leaning over to try to balance in the wind, they understood Jillian needed to hurry. They could hear her chanting but could not make out the words.

Chris worried about whether this plan was going to work. The power and energy created when the dark spirits opened the portal using so many amulets at one time could be very extreme. As he stood feeling more dread as every minute went by, James understood the situation was going to get much worse. He could hear the creatures rapidly moving up the well walls now. The noise of so many as they were screeching, growling, snarling, and scrambling up the walls. In seconds they were going to be expelled into our world- and then what? James felt the panic well up inside him.

Matt yelled, "Look out, they are coming out now!" The team was pushed down to the ground by the force of energy emerging from the well. They were all pressed towards the ground unable to move as thousands of creatures scrambled out of the well, around on the inside walls of the building, and over each team member stretched out on the floor. Jillian and Bella used their bodies to protect the items being used for the spell. It took significant effort to hold up their bodies as they worked against the energy pushing them down. Jillian lifted her head against the force of the pressure to see what was happening. She lifted her head only a couple of inches and it took great effort to open her eyes. She could see a mass of moving legs and arms with flashes of long gray wisps of hair. She could feel the long bony toes and fingers running across her back, legs, neck, and head. The long nails dug in through her clothes, piercing into her skin. At times, the pressure on her ribs from the weight of the creatures caused her to lose her breath. The creatures exploded out of the heavy wooden doors and into the world. Jillian reached over to add the final element to the pot of fire that was barely lit. Bella was struggling to hold the pot upright with her arms as she was stretched out flat on the floor. Jillian held the final element as she tried to place it in the pot. It was the feather. The final element to finish the spell. As she held it tightly the wind tried to carry it away. She felt the wind increase and as the creatures continued to pummel her, she found herself unable to move close enough to the pot. Jillian let out a scream as she lost her grip on the feather, and it was taken away by the wind. James heard her scream and could see the feather caught up in the wind. He lunged toward it and grabbed the edge. It was enough to take control of it and with heroic effort, he handed it back to Jillian. In one motion she added the feather to the ceramic container in the pot with the fire. It was done. By now the team was moaning and crying out in pain and languishing that the efforts may not have been enough to stop the scourge. All of this might have been for nothing.

Nick looked over at Aden. He was standing upright in the corner observing what was happening around him. He had a curious look about him that seemed to be absent of fear. Nick yelled to Matt, Chris, and James, "Look at Aden! He is untouched by all of this chaos!" They turned to see Aden standing upright, with no wind or chaos around him. No creatures running over him. He seemed to be standing within an area of complete calm.

As they observed Aden, he appeared enigmatic. The team watched him with incredulous intensity as the energy in the room changed. Just as Jillian and Bella had given up hope that the spell worked, they noticed the inside of the fire pot sparkling. Something was happening. The gusty wind moving all around them became more focused wind moving toward the well. Jillian yelled, "I think the spell is working!" As she said this the wind became more intense and it was so strong, that the team was moved forcefully toward the well. Chris yelled, "Hold on to something!" Bella held on to an iron part of the wall structure. Jillian could not find anything to hold on to, so Bella grabbed her arm. Chris, Matt, Angie, James, and Nick found parts of the walls to grab and hold. Aden continued to stand in the same place watching the scene play out.

The momentum of creatures moving out of the well, through the well building, and out the wooden doors began to change. The din created by the creatures became louder and more intense. It was the growling, snarling, and screeching of protest as the creatures were forced backwards toward the well. The scrambling became more confused as they tried to fight the energy sending them back toward the well and the portal. It became a desperate fight for survival as the creatures tried everything in their power to prevent the forced movement back. In the end, they were not powerful enough to fight the momentum.

The rush of wind knocked everyone down again. They struggled to stand as the energy and powerful gusts moved over and around them. The wind was so strong it caused the skin on their faces to blow and contort. Hair was being whipped around, and bright bursts of energy and light would spontaneously occur around them. They could hear the creatures approaching. The screaming, growling, and guttural noises coming from the creatures continued as they desperately tried to prevent the momentum from sending them back to purgatory. Clawing, grabbing anything around them to prevent the energy from sending them back. The horrible smell the creatures emitted was getting stronger as the masses grew closer. They were drawn together in a large moving mass of clawing, angry and desperate creatures. It was a scene of mayhem. Jillian could see the brilliant glow of the solid red aura surrounding this mass. The large moving mass approached closer to the portal in the well that would project them back to where they originated. A creature reached outside of the mass to grab a structure of the building, only to be pulled away and moved back into the mass by the energy, as it made a screaming noise in objection. At one point Jillian made eye contact with one of the creatures and it held her stare. It held her and it felt as though time stopped. She stared into the red eyes with the sloshing liquid. She could feel the hostility and the murderous intentions in its stare. She had difficulty breaking away feeling compelled to look at it. James yelled, "Don't look at them!" He pulled her arm so she would turn to look at him. James yelled, "They will try anything in this moment to stay."

Angie watched as Aden walked from the corner where he stood. He walked easily against the wind and toward the well and the portal. The mass of creatures was being forced down the well one at a time. They clawed and scraped at the stone walls surrounding the well as they were forced through. The now shrieking screams were so loud it was impossible for anyone to think or speak above the noise. One after one the creatures were forced back.

After some time passed, the mass of creatures dwindled. The thunderous noise decreased. As the last few were forced down the well and through the portal, the group heard a new deafening noise. The sound of pounding footsteps was so forceful the thumping caused the building to shake violently. The earthquake caused part of the building walls to give way. The team held on to whatever part of the structure they could find again, as the pounding grew louder, and the building shook more fiercely. Bella yelled, "This could be the leader!" They all braced themselves for what was coming next. The largest creature was coming. Probably the leader and the most powerful. They all wondered if the portal and the energy from the portal would be strong enough to push this powerful creature back. It began to scream a low, loud scream and then a low evil laugh. The laugh sent shivers down everyone's spine. Jillian turned to see this huge creature being dragged backward by the energy and the wind toward the portal. The red aura surrounding this creature was dynamic. There were bursts of bright energy within the aura. Then Nick spotted what it had in its hand. The third amulet. It was holding the third amulet that could be used to reverse this whole process and release all the creatures back into our world for good. It turned to look at Nick with a knowing look. Nick screamed, "Look out, it has the third amulet!" Aden had been frozen in one place again watching. He now turned around slowly and moved toward the creature. It laughed again, with a laugh that reverberated throughout everyone's bodies. Its large sunken eyes were glowing red with swishing liquid that spilled out around its face as the head moved. It had thin gray skin hanging from its head and body in tatters like the old wallpaper at thc Chateau. The long white hair hung in wisps exposing most of its gray head and skull. The creature was truly monstrous. It abruptly stopped, paused for a moment, and let out a horrible sound that was a combination of a laugh and a screech. Then it turned to look directly at Jillian. She made eye contact with it as it lifted its long bony arm and pointed at her with a long finger. It said in a low raspy voice that sounded like a noise directly from hell, "I am the one you want to speak with." She shivered at the sound of the creature's voice as well as the words. This was the creature that had been trying to communicate with her all of this time. Through the prisoner, the Barrington brother who died in the car accident on the cliff, and the creature in her dream. It made sense now. It was trying to acquire the amulets and it knew they had one from the previous Edin house investigation.

The creature opened its other hand to expose the missing piece of the third amulet. It moved its long skeletal hands and fingers to place the two pieces of the amulet back together. James panicked while watching the creature. He understood what it was trying to do. James tried to think of a way to prevent it from placing the amulet pieces back together. They had only seconds. It was trying to reverse the energy that would send the thousands of evil creatures back into our world and close the portal.

Its nails were long and yellowed and placing the pieces of the amulet together proved to be cumbersome. The seconds of time it took for the creature to place the pieces of the amulet together gave Aden the moment he needed. Aden unexpectedly jumped in front of it and grabbed the amulet pieces before they were placed back together. The creature screamed and swiped aggressively at Aden. It was still held back by the energy and momentum toward the portal and could not effectively fight Aden. As it moved toward him the team gasped in unison. The creature moved closer to Aden and before it could grab him, it was picked up again by the energy and moved toward the well. The creature's movement gained momentum and it was moving faster toward the well and the portal. Aden stayed close as the creature screamed and moaned, scratching and clawing to get away. As it was pushed through the portal the stone wall broke away by the force and Aden turned to look at Angie.

He stood with the wind whipping around his hair, the energy and lights bursting around him. She yelled, "No! Aden don't do it!" Bella said under her breath, "Oh no, please don't." As Bella spoke, for a moment time stopped. The wind blew Aden's hair away from his face and she noticed a black mark that was starkly visible on Aden's head next to his ear. Bella recognized this mark, and she moved her hair away from the side of her face to rub the two marks she had in the same spot. She was born with these black marks, and he had one that looked the same.

Jillian screamed above the noise as Aden said in a calm voice, "It's ok. I believe this is why I have these gifts. I never understood it until now. This is what I am intended to do. This is how I am supposed to use my abilities. Don't worry about me. This is what fate intended for me." As he said this Jillian noticed the brilliant green aura surrounding him. She could see he was genuinely at peace amidst the chaos. Jillian and James looked at one another and she said, "Let's help him." James took her hand, and they closed their eyes to focus and concentrate. They focused their combined energy to help to push back the creatures scrambling to be released again. Aden watched them and took that moment to quickly turn and run toward the well and the portal holding the two pieces of the amulet. He jumped into the well without looking back. There was an explosive sound and then a fireball erupted and grew out of the well. The fire became expansive, and the group had to kneel and look away as the heat and wind became too much. In the midst of the chaos, James and Jillian felt the energy and force created between them and continued to concentrate, focusing on keeping the energy from flowing back toward them from the portal. They needed to create a barrier to prevent the creatures from crawling back through during the brief moments when the portal was closing. They were not sure they could help but were committed to trying, using the knowledge and experience they possessed. The fireball rose and within the intense fire, two of the amulets were expelled -broken into four pieces. The pieces landed on the ground scattered around them. Jillian and James were plunged to the ground by the strength of the wind and fire. The energy bond and force between them were broken. After a few moments, the wind and energy died down, the portal closed, and the environment surrounding the team eventually became quiet and calm.

Chapter 19

Acceptance

James, Jillian, Nick, Matt, Angie, Bella, and Chris sat on the floor looking at one another. Angie spoke through tears, "Aden sacrificed himself to save us all. He is now stuck in purgatory forever." The tears were flowing. Nick walked over to Angie, and she placed her head on his shoulder. The loss was hard for them to fully grasp at that moment. James found himself wondering if there might be a way to rescue Aden. Maybe they could find a way to bring him back. But what would he be like if they did? Would he be forever changed like the other creatures? It was a terrible thought.

They stood up and realized the outbuilding structure that once surrounded them was gone. The well was sealed and closed off completely by a large pile of stones from the well walls that collapsed. They were looking up at the clear night sky. For the first time since they had arrived at Susurrous Pines, it seemed very peaceful. The feeling of unrest, anxiety and impending doom had been lifted. They could hear the wind blowing through the majestic pines. The soft whirring noise it created added to the calm. It was clear that for now, the evil and the darkness that had blanketed this town appeared to be banished.

Chris looked down and saw the four pieces of the broken amulets. He pointed at them and said, "Look, we still have two of the amulets. Aden must have found a way to eject the pieces through the portal as it was closing. He did not want the creatures to have another opportunity to use them." James said, "I hope that Aden can keep a safe hold on the third amulet. I pray he is strong enough to maintain his humanity in that place to prevent the dark spirits from gaining access to that amulet and start creating portals again." Angie whispered, "I have faith in him. He is the strongest person I have ever met." Bella rubbed the side of her head where the black birthmarks were. She did not feel at peace at the moment. She now had a secret. A secret she did not understand and felt she could not discuss with the group yet. She felt a strong loyalty to each team member and felt as if she was violating trust. Deep down she understood the importance of her discovery. She and Aden share something Bella did not understand. These marks she was born with could be a gift, or they might be a curse. Could her birthmarks be the key to her innate and internal struggles? She felt completely overcome and intensely compelled to find answers.

They started the walk back to the Chateau. Matt was limping and Chris asked if he was injured. Matt answered, "A large stone hit my leg, but I think it is only bruised. Jillian was still very sore around her shoulders from her previous injuries. Chris and Bella still wore bandages from the assault by the creatures. They all suffered from many cuts, abrasions, and bruising. It was all minor compared to the sacrifices Aden made.

The team went back to the rooms to pack and organize before leaving. Angie went to her room and packed up her gear. The team had accumulated hours of video and recordings from the entirety of the investigation. The pace of the Susurrous Pines investigation was so rapid they did not have time to review and study all the footage. This would have to wait until a later date. Maybe something they find from the video and tapes could help them with future investigations. When her gear was packed, she walked over to Aden's room. She had volunteered to pack up his things.

Angie opened the door to Aden's room and stood in the doorway for a moment looking around the room as he had left it. An open bag on the bed, and a book open on the nightstand. She found a jacket on the chair and placed it in the bag. She walked over to pick up the book from the nightstand. Closing it she glanced at the title. The book was titled, "Apex One- The New Horizon: How to Help Spirits Move On." Angie read the inside flap as well as the information on the back of the book. It was written by two mediums with reported experience helping spirits who might be resistant or stuck and unable to move on. Spirits who might not understand they have died, or who have unresolved issues and feel compelled to stay. Aden had written notes in the front of the book. Unfinished notes that read like instructions in list form. She realized he wished to help those spirits like Flannery Token and perhaps the children and others who died in the mining accident. He had previously mentioned feeling a connection to the dark spirits after his experience in the tunnels. He must have also developed a connection with the other benevolent spirits in that realm. She was touched by his apparent desire to help them move on. Angie wondered if he might be able to help them now that he crossed over and was sharing that space. She felt uplifted thinking about this additional way he might be able to help others. It reinforced for her his positive intentions and attempt to use his abilities for good. Her heart ached with the loss and somehow at the same time, she felt comforted having discovered this new information. She continued to pack up his personal items and came across his phone. The cover photo on his phone was a picture of the team. They were smiling together sitting on the front steps of Chris's estate. A happier time.

The team met outside in front of the Chateau to load the cars. It was late afternoon by now and Mags was trotting around them getting underfoot as they loaded. Everyone was quiet, and the mood was sad and morose. Jillian said, "We should be celebrating the success of closing the portals and banishing the creatures, and instead we are mourning the loss of Aden." "It shouldn't have gone this way." Angie said, "Aden made a choice. It was very brave of him, and I will never forget it." Matt limped up to the car and grabbed his bag. He took out shot glasses and a bottle of vodka. He announced, "Let's toast to Aden." They poured the shots and held the glasses to the sky. "Matt said, "To Aden, we will never forget what you did for us and humanity. You are a hero. You are our hero." They drank the shots and stayed quiet for a while. Time passed and it was almost sunset. The group decided it was time to leave.

Chris and Bella were using a rental car obtained last minute due to the state of the wrecked car. They had arranged for a tow truck to take the wrecked car to the nearby garage for assessment and possible repairs. They would manage the details long distance from the estate. Bella and Chris needed to leave Susurrous Pines with the team.

Jillian loaded up the car with Mags in the back. She opened the back hatch to load a few more bags as Mags peered over the back seat watching. Jillian spotted the locked container that held Russ. She impulsively grabbed the box and unlocked it to find Russ still inside. She quickly closed the box and locked it. She would need to find a new safe place for it. Maybe Chris would allow her to keep it locked away at the estate. For now, she quickly stashed it underneath the bags in the back of the car.

Jillian glanced at James and turned to look at the Chateau one more time before getting in the car. She noticed a large tree positioned at the side of the Chateau near the covered porch. There was an ominous-looking dark shadow on the thick trunk of this tree. The shadow was in the shape of a hooded figure crouched over. It looked like the last drawing on the wall in the staircase room leading to the tunnels. She felt the wave of adrenaline and panic set in for a moment. She whispered, "James, do you see the shadow on the trunk of that tree?" He looked at her and followed where she was looking. He did not see anything. Jillian closed her eyes, looked again, and it was gone. She saw a tree trunk and nothing unusual. Did she imagine it? James asked if she was all right. Jillian sighed and said she was tired, and her mind was playing tricks on her. She looked around and noticed an oddly shaped bird feeder and decided the bird feeder must have been the source of the shadow. The setting sun casting long shadows on the tree trunks nearby. This was an easy conclusion to choose. She had not completely shaken off the creepiness and constant fear of the recent days. She could attribute her imagination and the creativity of her subconscious to the impact of the recent intense experiences. This was a much better option. She could not allow herself to consider the alternative after everything they had been through. Jillian laughed at herself for being ridiculous and moved on.

One by one they drove the cars down the long driveway away from the Chateau. They drove by the wrecked car still resting next to the tree they hit. The windows were smashed and the front end and sides were extremely damaged. Chris commented the car would most likely be a total loss and they were fortunate not to be more seriously injured.

Bella and Chris were the last to drive across the covered bridge leaving town, and Bella asked him to stop on the other side. She got out of the car and watched as the fog drifted over and enveloped the bridge until it disappeared completely. She looked to her right and could see Jillian and James standing outside of their car. Angie was also standing outside of her car a short distance away. Bella waved to all of them in acknowledgment. The four looked around and surveyed the beautiful mountains and landscape surrounding the town. It was a bittersweet departure. Jillian and James believed they would be returning to Susurrous Pines someday. They stood leaning on the car. James took Jillian's hand and kissed it gently while Mags, standing on the back seat watched them through the window of the car with her tail wagging.

Standing in front of the bridge on the edge of town, Angie experienced great reluctance about leaving. Leaving town felt as though she was separating from Aden forever. In her mind, it was like she was abandoning him. Realistically she understood there was nothing more she could do for him at this time, and she was struggling with coming to terms with the permanency of his loss. She flinched when thinking about where he ended up and what tortures he might be enduring. Angie closed her eyes and remembered that final image of him with the wind, the dramatic flashes of light, and his hair blowing in front of his face. He stood strong in the face of evil and adversity with a sense of courage, confidence, and purpose. This image gave her the strength to turn and step back into the car.

Bella also hesitated. She inhaled and exhaled a long breath and took in the vista one more time before getting back in the car. Once in the car she rolled down the window, closed her eyes, and listened to the wind blowing peacefully through the pines. She understood her future direction started now with the path immediately in front of her. Where they will go, and what the future holds is a mixture of elements including life experience, circumstance, fate, and the ability to make choices. Aden believed in all of these elements and had the courage to make a choice regarding his purpose. He saved them in the process. She caught a glimpse in the side view mirror of the marks next to her ear. She lightly touched the marks and then pulled her hair over to cover them. She sighed before turning and looking straight ahead. Chris asked, "Are you ready?" Bella answered, "I am now." They pulled out behind the other cars and started the drive up the mountain road. The fiery sunset of yellow, red, orange, and pink glowed through the blue and purple clouds displaying brilliant streams of light between the mountains, through the fog in the valley, and the vast forest. The world was safe again... for now.

The End

Made in the USA
Monee, IL
06 September 2023

42257212R00096